I0715776

The

TASTE

of an

ENEMY

The TASTE of an ENEMY

HOLLY RENEE

The Taste of an Enemy

Copyright © 2021 by Holly Renee.
All rights reserved.

No part of this book may be reproduced in any form or by any electronic or mechanical means, including information storage and retrieval systems, without written permission from the author, except for the use of brief quotations in a book review.

This is a work of fiction. Names, characters, businesses, places, events, and incidents are either the products of the author's imagination or used in a fictional manner. Any resemblance to actual persons, living or deceased, or events is purely coincidental.

Cover Designer: Brittany Keller Art
Editor: Ellie McLove
Proofread: Rumi Khan
www.authorhollyrenee.com

FOR CARSON

Who thinks he should be on the cover of every romance novel I write.

This one is for you, Casanova.

CHAPTER 1

CARSON

I fucking loved Halloween parties.

What wasn't to love? Almost every girl here was dressed sluttier than I had ever seen them. Everyone was drinking, and my chances of getting laid tonight were pretty damn high.

The slutty nurse sitting on my lap right now was proof of that. Everything was perfect. My ideal night.

Until Allie Taylor walked through the damn door dressed like a cowgirl who could never possibly ride a horse. Her rhinestone cowboy boots went up to her knees, and her shorts barely covered her ass. There was a black cowboy hat resting on the top of her head and a pink bandana around her neck that did nothing to hide her tits that were practically busting out of her top.

Frankie and Josie were both dressed similarly, but I could barely see them because Allie was so distracting.

How the hell did Beck let them walk out of the house like that?

"What the hell are you supposed to be?" I asked them all,

but I was looking directly at Allie. For the life of me, I couldn't fucking quit looking at her.

"We're rhinestone cowgirls." She grinned and adjusted her bandana.

I knew I should have just left her alone, but I couldn't. It was either be cruel to her or fuck her. Those were the only two thoughts I had when it came to Allie. It was all I had been able to think about for years, and there was no way we were going there, so cruel it was.

"You look like a slut with a cowboy hat."

Her face fell, and my chest ached for the smallest moment. But I forced that shit to go away. I hated Allie, hated her, and the sadness on her face wasn't going to change that.

I refused to let it.

"You are such an asshole, Carson." This came from Frankie, and she wasn't wrong. I was being an asshole. Allie looked beautiful, too beautiful, and it was driving me crazy.

There was no way in hell I was telling them that, so instead I simply shrugged my shoulders with a fake-ass grin on my face.

Allie's gaze slid away from me and moved to where my hand rested on the nurse's hip. I didn't even know her name. I knew how horrible that sounded, but I preferred it that way. Because I had no plans with this girl beyond tonight.

I never did.

"Do you have an issue?" the nurse asked Allie, but I wished for once she would just stand up and say that she did. I wished she would say exactly what was going on in that head of hers, but she never did when it came to me.

Not anymore.

Not since we were kids.

"I do." Frankie raised her hand and moved in front of me. She cut off my view of Allie, and I wanted to push her out of the way. I loved Frankie, but God, I just wanted to stare at Allie. I wanted to watch her be upset by the fact that there was another girl on my lap.

Frankie moved to my lap and sat down on the opposite knee from the nurse. She wasn't gentle, and almost squashed my balls as she forced herself closer to me and forced the nurse out. The girl looked back at me, but there was no way I would deny Frankie. Not after everything that girl had been through.

"Are you kidding me?" She was waiting for me to push Frankie away, but I didn't.

She stood, her fine ass swaying as she stomped away from me, and Frankie shooed her away with her hand like she was a dog.

I wrapped my arms around Frankie and nuzzled into the back of her neck. "You're such a cock-block, you know that?"

"I do." She patted my thigh. "But you're a slut. You didn't need that girl tonight."

"Wow, Frankie." I chuckled against her just as Olly and Beck walked up behind the girls. I hadn't seen any of them all night. "Tell me how you really feel."

Frankie was beautiful too, but she was innocent. She was one of my best friend's baby sister, and sometimes I felt like Olly and I were more protective of her than Beck was. But there were other times, like right now, when Olly was staring daggers at my head like he wanted to kill me, that I thought maybe Olly felt more for this girl.

But it was something that would never happen.

Not after what Lucas had done to her.

Beck would never forgive Olly for going there. Never.

Olly knew that too. It was why he caught himself and looked away before anyone noticed that tortured look on his face, but I noticed. I always did.

"Come on, girls. Let's go get a drink." Josie wrapped her arm in Allie's as she stared daggers at me, and I hugged Frankie tighter against me one last time before she climbed off my lap and walked away.

"I swear to God, you have to be the biggest idiot sometimes." Beck ran his fingers through his hair as he watched his girl walk away.

"I know." We had this conversation multiple times before. He and Olly both thought I was too harsh on Allie. They thought I just had a boner for the girl, but that wasn't it at all. They didn't know Allie like I did. They had no fucking clue what happened between us. "But I wasn't wrong."

"Every girl here is dressed like that, but you just had to say something to Allie, right?"

"I can't help it that she was the first one I saw." I shrugged.

"Or that she was the only one you couldn't quit eye-fucking." Olly shook his head. "I wish the two of you would just have it out and get it over with."

"Not going to happen, my man." I stood and patted him on the shoulder before I passed them to get a drink. I needed one, desperately.

A few of the players on our baseball team were gathered around a bottle of dark liquor laughing, and I quickly snatched it up before I took a long drag. "What the hell are you all up to?"

I liked most of my teammates, thought of most of them as brothers, except for Josie's stepbrother, Lucas, and his idiot friends. I fucking hated them.

"We've got a bet going." Seth, our center fielder, had the biggest damn grin on his face.

"A bet about what? I'm sure Vos is destined to lose." I patted Lucas on the chest and watched the anger rise in his eyes.

"You want to join?" He shook the baseball cap that was in his hands. There were dozens of folded-up pieces of paper inside.

"What are we betting on?" I matched his stare because there was no way in hell I was willing to back down from this asshole.

"Getting the girl." He cocked his head to the side, and there was so much challenge in his stare.

"You all need to make a bet to get a girl?" I looked around at my teammates. "I thought most of you had better game than that."

"Oh, we have plenty of game, but these girls are the ultimate challenge."

It was on the tip of my tongue to remind Lucas exactly what he had done in the past. I wanted to throw it in his face what a piece of shit he was, but he already knew. We both did, and bringing it up here would do nothing but hurt Frankie.

"So, what? We just have to get the girl? Make her like us?" This sounded pretty fucking lame to me.

"Make her like you. Fuck her. All before fall break."

"Damn." I chuckled. "You all need that long to get a girl in bed?"

Lucas stuck the hat out in my direction. "Draw a name, Hale."

I shook my head as I thought about their idiotic plan. "No, thank you. I don't need to play your little games to get pussy. I've got that handled." I winked at Lucas and a couple of the guys laughed.

"Suit yourself." He dropped it so easily, far too easily, before he moved around the group and let everyone draw a name.

He stopped directly in front of me and drew his own name out of the hat. There was only one sheet of paper left, and he pushed the hat back in my direction.

"Not happening."

He shrugged his shoulders before moving on to his buddy, Eli. Eli reached inside and opened the paper with a giant grin on his face.

"Frankie's name better not be in that fucking pile, Lucas."

He held up his hands innocently. "Never."

Then I watched in horror as the boys all started showing off who they got. Eli turned his paper around, the paper that Lucas had meant for me, and I stared down at Allie's name.

"That's not fucking happening." I tried to grab her name from Eli, but he quickly moved it out of my reach.

"Yes. It is." He tucked her name into his pocket as if that would somehow make a difference. "I've been dying for a chance to get a piece of her sweet ass for years. Did you see it practically hanging out of her shorts tonight?"

I lunged at him before I even had time to think about what I was doing, but far too many guys jumped in to stop me.

"Give me her fucking name, Eli."

"Hell no." This one came from Lucas. "You said you didn't want to play."

"I changed my mind. I'm in, and I want Allie's name." I would do anything to keep her from being a part of this. I could just picture her with Eli, falling for his stupid fucking charm.

"Too late." Lucas grinned and someone pushed against my chest to force me to back up. "I gave you multiple opportunities to participate, but you don't need help with pussy. Remember?"

I was going to kill Lucas. He used to be my friend, one of my best friends, and he was one of the only people who knew about what happened between me and Allie. He was one of the only ones who knew that I used to be head over heels in love with the girl.

"Lucas, I'm not fucking around."

He stepped up, his face just inches from my own, and I should have pummeled him right then and there. "I'm not either. It's Eli's job to get in Allie's pants now. I think you should probably give up after all these years."

"You're not going to touch her." I stared at Eli, and I could practically feel his fear. Good. That meant he knew I wasn't fucking around. He wasn't going to touch her. Not if I had any say in it. Not if I could stop him.

"There's nothing you can do to stop him." Lucas laughed and moved away from me. "Allie has hated you for years after how mean you've been to her. She won't listen to you if you try to warn her. She'll just think you're being the same cruel asshole you've always been."

He was right. Fuck. Both of us knew it. If I told Allie that Eli was only into her for a bet, she would absolutely think I was just being a dick. The girls would too. They had watched me be an ass to her time and time again. I wouldn't blame them. I would think the exact same thing.

But as much as I hated Allie, I couldn't sit back and watch her get hurt or humiliated by them. Lucas and his boys were nothing but douchebags, and Eli was one of the worst.

I may have been cruel to Allie, but I would never really hurt her. I would never do the things that I knew Lucas was capable of. I didn't know if Eli was capable of those things too, but I wasn't about to sit back and find out.

"Then I'll make her fall for me."

Lucas laughed along with half the guys standing around us, and my heart felt like it was trying to beat out of my chest.

"If that's what it takes to keep you all away from her, then that's what I'll do."

"Allie will never fall for you, dude." Lucas took a long swig of liquor. "It's a losing battle."

She wouldn't, but I still had to try. If I could convince Allie to fall for me, to spend time with me, then I could keep her as far away from these assholes as possible. Then that was what I would do.

"Then I guess you all have yourselves a bet."

CHAPTER 2
ALLIE

Carson Hale was the biggest asshole I had ever met.

He had been for a long time. For far too long. He had been this way ever since he decided that he no longer wanted to be my friend.

Because we were friends once upon a time, whether he wants to remember it that way or not, and he was the one who decided that what we were was over.

He made that decision, and I lost my best friend and the boy I had been secretly in love with all in one day.

Now he hated me.

And he made sure to take every possible opportunity to remind me of that fact.

I could usually deal with it. I had learned a long time ago to just let his comments roll off my back like they didn't even matter, but it was becoming so much harder these days. It wasn't just his comments either. It was watching him parade around with any girl he could get his hands on like he was constantly throwing them in my face.

I knew how ludicrous that was.

He didn't care about me. He sure as hell wasn't worried about making me jealous.

But it felt that way. I felt like every move he made was a deliberate act to get under my skin. It was something he had become very good at too.

Because I was jealous. I didn't even know who the hell Carson was anymore, but I was still jealous of every one of those girls who got to know him. Who got to have a piece of him that I would never have.

That I never got the chance to have.

I lifted the shot Josie just handed me and pressed it to my lips. The liquor burned, but it also eased the deep ache in my chest. At least a little. I couldn't believe that he said I looked like a slut.

Not only were Josie and Frankie dressed almost identical to me tonight, but we were also the most modestly dressed girls at the entire party. The girl that had been on his lap had on less fabric than my bra and panties, and he had the nerve to say I looked like a slut.

I grabbed the liquor bottle and filled the shot glass again.

I could see the concern in Josie's eyes and the way she kept looking at Frankie. They thought I was likely to snap, and they weren't wrong. I could feel my blood boiling, every bit of hate I had for Carson spilling over the edge.

I threw back the next shot as I avoided her gaze and looked around the party. Everyone was having a blast. The music was blaring through the speakers, people were dancing and grinning, and I hated that Carson had put me in a bad mood.

"Come on." Frankie grabbed my hand in hers and pulled me to the center of the living room. "Let's go dance."

There was no way I could refuse her. Instead, I followed behind her and tried to plant a smile on my face to match hers, and I let her twirl me around in a circle before a genuine smile took over.

"You're a terrible dancer," I yelled the lie over the music, but it made her smile bigger.

"That's what I hear." She shimmied her chest in my direction before finding the beat of the music. "But they say terrible dancers are really good in bed, right?"

"I have no idea." I shrugged. Frankie and I were probably the only two girls at this party who were still virgins. "Your guess is as good as mine."

Frankie started doing a super awkward hip-thrusting move that was drawing way too much attention, but I couldn't quit laughing. She didn't stop either. Not until I was clenching my belly and had almost completely forgotten about Carson.

Because that was the kind of friend she was.

"Hey there, cowgirls."

Frankie and I both stopped laughing and looked up at Eli Scott. I knew who he was because almost everyone did, but I had never spoken to him before.

"Hi," Frankie said dismissively and reached out for my hand.

But Eli's attention stayed on me. "It's Allie, right?"

"Yeah." I nodded as I answered.

"I thought so." He grinned, and I had to admit that it did something to his face that made him even more handsome than before. "If your girl wouldn't mind me cutting in, I'd love to dance with you."

As soon as the words passed his lips, a much slower song with a heavy beat rang through the speakers. Frankie squeezed my hand. I didn't know if she was telling me to say no or yes, but I knew what I wanted to say.

"I'd love to."

I pulled my hand away from Frankie's and placed it in Eli's outreached one. He tugged me toward him gently until my chest pressed against his, and I let my body move with his to the music. He was much better at this than I would have guessed.

"I love your costume, by the way." He tipped the front of my cowgirl hat with the tip of his finger before he let it trail down my back and rest there.

"Thank you." I smiled, but I couldn't keep the thoughts of what Carson had to say about it at bay. Here I was dancing with this guy who was far too attractive for his own good, and I was still thinking about what Carson had said. "And what exactly are you supposed to be?"

I leaned away from him slightly so I could get a good look at his costume. He was dressed in a dark dress suit with a vest included, and he wore a flat cap on his head that covered most of his sandy brown hair.

"Thomas Shelby." He looked down at me like I was supposed to somehow know who that was. "From *Peaky Blinders*."

"I've never seen it." I shrugged, and he pressed one of his hands into his chest.

"It's only the best show ever." He sounded offended that I hadn't seen it. "I guess I know exactly what we're going to have to do on our first date."

My stomach flipped at his words, and I couldn't stop the stupid grin that I knew was taking over my face. Eli Scott was hot, and I didn't know how to react to him suddenly being interested in me. "I don't remember agreeing to a date."

"Are you sure?" He cocked his head to the side and pulled me in closer to him so our bodies were touching.

He was staring down at me like I had never been looked at before. I didn't have much experience when it came to guys, but I knew one thing for sure. The look he was giving me was one of want. Having someone look at me with such an open and easy desire was overwhelming and so attractive.

"I could have sworn you just asked me to introduce you to *Peaky Blinders*."

"What if I hate it?" I asked as he continued to sway us to the music.

"Then we'll have to end it right then and there. We could never go on after that." He was so playful and charming, and I felt light dancing in his arms.

"I feel the same way about *Gilmore Girls*, you know?"

He curled his top lip, and I laughed. "Does that mean we're going to have to binge-watch it after *Peaky Blinders*?"

"Only if you plan on getting serious," I joked because I knew that nothing was probably going to come of this after tonight, but it was nice to pretend.

Just for a few minutes, I could imagine myself curled up on a couch with him watching whatever he wanted to watch and begging my heart to slow down. I wanted that. I wanted it far more than I realized.

"It's a date then." He stepped back as the song ended and brought my hand to his mouth. He pressed a gentle kiss to the back of my hand and winked at me. "Next Tuesday, we'll meet up at six."

"Okay." I nodded as I stared at my hand that was still near his mouth.

He pulled his phone out of his pocket and handed it to me.

"Give me your number so I can text you."

I typed it in without hesitation, then watched as he typed in Gorgeous Cowgirl before saving it.

"I'll let you get back to your friends." He nodded over my shoulder, and when I turned around, I spotted the entire group along the edge of the room, including Carson. He was staring daggers at the two of us, but I attempted to avoid his gaze altogether. Eli pushed my hair over my right shoulder as he leaned forward and whispered, "I'll see you on Tuesday."

Goose bumps trailed down my arms. Then just like that, he was gone.

"Excuse me, but he's hot." Josie was watching me as I stepped up beside her.

Carson scoffed, but I ignored him.

"He is." I couldn't stop smiling. "He's charming too."

"You girls have really poor taste in men." Olly rolled his eyes at us.

"I'm dating your best friend, remember?" Josie asked.

"I do" —Olly nodded his head dramatically— "and he's about as charming as a wet noodle."

"I can hear you, asshole." Beck was far from offended. Instead, he wrapped his arms around Josie and nuzzled his face into her neck. From the details Josie had shared with me, Beck was more than charming.

"It seems that you have really poor taste in friends then, Olly, because you've somehow managed to pick two charmers." Olly laughed at my comment, but Carson didn't. Instead, he cocked his head to the side and studied me. I tried to avoid looking at him at all, but he was so unnerving.

"You picked me as your friend once upon a time too, remember?"

I was shocked by his comment. Carson had said plenty to me over the years, but he never brought up the past. I had almost convinced myself that we didn't have one.

"I do." I nodded and memories of us bombarded me. Memories of how much I used to care for him and how close we used to be. It was the memories of him that made me feel anything at all for him anymore. "And look how that ended for me."

I could feel everyone watching us, but suddenly, I didn't care. I was desperate for Carson to say something more, to be mean if that's all he was capable of. I just needed something more.

He had become a master of hiding his emotions, and I used to be able to read them so well. I would give anything to be able to see past that mask he wore these days.

"You ended up exactly where you wanted to be, Allie." His fingers skimmed over his jaw as he talked to me, and I couldn't stop myself from watching every inch of the movement. "Don't forget that you're the one who put yourself there."

He was so full of crap. I didn't put myself anywhere. I was his friend, I was in love with him, and he had dropped me like I was nothing.

"That's not how I remember things." I balled my hand into a fist. "But of course, that's how you do. You've never done anything wrong in your life, Carson. Have you?"

"Besides ever wasting my time on you?" He looked up at the ceiling like he was thinking and hadn't just wounded me to my core. "No. I don't think so."

"I hate you." I stared him straight in the eyes as I said it, and I meant it. This guy, this Carson that stood in front of me, he was nothing like the boy I used to know.

There was a flash in Carson's eyes, but I couldn't figure out what it was. It couldn't be regret and I knew that my words didn't hurt him, but there was something. It was there one moment and then it was gone. "Ditto, baby."

CHAPTER 3

CARSON

Allie had left hours ago, and I still couldn't stop thinking about how stupid I had been. Being cruel to her was going to do nothing but push her directly into Eli's arms, but I had been so angry when I saw him touching her. When I saw how pliable she had been under his hands.

Then she turned around and had that stupid fucking look on her face like he had just shown her the best time of her life. I wanted to pummel him, but more than that, I wanted to punish her. I wanted to ruin that moment she just had. I wanted her to hate it as much as I did.

So I pushed her like I always did, and I forced her to hate me. That was the only thing I was good at when it came to her.

But it wasn't what I needed.

Guys like Eli and Lucas. They would ruin Allie, and as much as I hated her, I couldn't let that happen. I couldn't be that cruel even if she already thought I was.

Even though Allie had hurt me once upon a time, I

couldn't let them hurt her. Not like this. Allie was mine to fuck with.

She was mine.

That irrational thought played over and over in my head.

She was the furthest thing from what I wanted but somehow, she was still all I could think about. Even now, with the fine-ass nurse from earlier pressed against my body and kissing up my neck. Allie was all I could think about.

It was infuriating.

I dug my fingers into her hip and tried to concentrate on what she was doing. It felt good. Fuck, she felt good, but it also felt wrong. It always did.

After all the girls I had been with, it was never enough.

None of them were ever enough.

But they were enough of a distraction that I normally didn't care. I need it. To distract my mind from everything that was going on around me.

From school. From my family. From her.

It never lasted long. There was only a small moment when I wasn't thinking of her. Then the girls' hair would remind me of Allie or remind me of how different she was. It was frustrating as hell.

I didn't want to think about her.

If I could completely erase her from my mind, I would.

And that was exactly what I was trying to do now.

"Do you like that?" the girl mumbled against my skin, and the sound of her voice grated on my nerves.

"Yeah." I gripped her arms in my hands and pulled her fully into my lap.

She moaned as her pussy pressed down against my erection. There was very little fabric separating the two of us, and I knew that she could feel exactly how hard I was.

I wanted her even though I didn't. I just needed her body, her escape, a fucking moment away from the constant bullshit in my head.

She ground down against me, and I leaned back in the chair. We were alone in someone's room, I had no fucking clue whose, and I could do anything I wanted to this girl.

Anything.

I knew that and so did she. She was eager and willing to let me do things to her body that I would probably remember for a very long time.

It was my idea of heaven.

Except I couldn't turn off my fucking mind.

At least that was what I told myself, but the reality was that I wouldn't think about her again after tonight. It felt like heaven and hell. She was nothing more than a quick distraction, a temporary high.

Her lips were full, but they weren't as full as Allie's. Her hair was brown and shiny, but Allie's was so blonde that it seemed to attract the sun. It always had been.

I reached up and ran my fingers through her hair, gripping the strands right at the base. She leaned her head back with a seductive smile on her face. She was right there, completely open for me, and still, I hesitated.

She moved against me harder, my cock was about to kill me if I didn't do something to her, but I just sat there. I let her ride against me through our clothes, and I held her hair firmly in my hands. She didn't seem to mind. Her eyes were glazed over with want, and I knew if I touched her, she'd be soaking wet against me.

She pressed her hands to my shoulders and held on as she brought her mouth down next to mine. "What do you want, baby?"

There should have been a thousand things on my mind in that moment. I should have given her all the ways I wanted to fuck her around this room, but I couldn't.

All I could think about was the way Allie had been smiling at Eli, and how I knew he was going to want to put her in this same position. He was going to want to fuck Allie like she was nameless and didn't matter.

And I fucking hated that.

I knew that was exactly what I was doing to this girl. But it felt different.

I knew how fucked up that was, but it was true.

Allie wasn't a virgin. I was almost one hundred percent positive of that fact. But I had rarely seen her show interest in any guy. She hadn't dated anyone that I was aware of.

And Eli fucking Scott wasn't going to be the guy who she thought would be her knight in shining armor.

I refused to allow it.

I wouldn't be either, but I could keep her as far away from him as possible.

But he was already a thousand steps ahead of me. He made her smile, and I saw her put her number into his phone. And she didn't fucking hate him.

That part was going to be tricky.

I shifted my hips and pulled my cell phone out of my pocket.

"What are you doing?"

I looked up from my phone at the girl who was still grinding against me. I held up a finger as I pushed myself out from under her. "Give me just a minute."

It was after two in the morning, and I was almost certain that Allie was probably already in bed. But I still clicked on her name. I hadn't called or text Allie in years. It felt odd.

But I refused to allow Eli to have the complete upper hand tonight.

I typed out a message to her, then erased it, then typed another. I did this over and over again as I thought about what to say to her.

I lied about you looking like a slut. You looked really hot tonight.

I hit Send before I could think better of it.

Her response came through my phone within a minute.

Who is this?

I grinned because she knew exactly who this was. Neither one of us had changed our phone numbers since we first convinced our parents to get us a phone when we were thirteen. Unless she had deleted my number. Shit. She might have done that.

Was there anyone else who was a complete ass to you tonight besides me?

Let me know and I'll kick their ass.

The three little dots danced across my screen before they disappeared. Then they started dancing again.

"Carson, can't that wait?"

I ignored the girl behind me and stared down at my phone.

Nope. Just you.

I don't know what you want but leave me alone.

I just wanted you to know how good you looked.

I should have apologized for saying she looked like a slut, but I rarely apologized for anything, and I never apologized to her.

Don't worry. Someone else already told me.

My anger was instant. I was telling her how slutty she looked while Eli was telling her the opposite. She didn't need me to tell her. She didn't need me to be anything for her.

Eli is a douchebag.

Her next response was instant.

Says the biggest douchebag I know. Do you need something, Carson?

No. I was just trying to be nice.

Well, don't. It's weird and giving me whiplash.

I grinned at her sass. It was one of the things that I had loved most about her once upon a time. It usually pissed me off now.

Noted. Back to being an asshole, I go.

She didn't respond after that, and I knew I should have put my phone down and left it at that. But I couldn't.

So I sent one last text message before I clicked off my phone and slid it back into my pocket.

Don't date Eli.

Then I turned around and faced the girl who was still waiting for me.

"I'm going to have to run." I ran my hand over the back of my neck.

"You have somewhere you need to be in the middle of the night?" She didn't believe a word I said.

"I do. A friend needs me."

"Is that why you were grinning down at your phone? I'm a big girl, Carson." She stood and grabbed her shoes from the floor. "You can just say that you're going to fuck someone else."

"All right." I shrugged my shoulders. "I'm going to fuck someone else." I was such a damn asshole.

She may have cared as little about me as I did her, but her face still fell when the words left my mouth.

"I can't believe you." She passed by me and headed straight for the door.

I didn't waste time as I followed her out. I needed to get out of this house. It smelled of beer and sex, and there were far too many bodies passed out on almost any available surface.

"Do you need a ride home?"

She turned around and stared at me like I had lost my damn mind. Maybe I had.

"I'm not letting my parents see me pull up to the house with Carson Hale," she snarled, her nose up, and I should have been offended but I knew she was pissed. I really didn't give a damn what her or her parents thought about me.

"Suit yourself." I pulled my keys out of my pocket and headed straight for the driveway.

I really didn't want to go home, though. My fucking parents were there, and even though they were probably asleep, I didn't want to deal with them. I never wanted to deal with them.

Not anymore.

Not after everything the two of them had done to each other.

I pulled my phone out of my pocket and text Beck.

Cool if I come over?

His text was instant and always the same.

Of course.

I tended to spend more time at his place or Olly's, and both of them knew why. If my parents weren't fighting, they were gone. Gone with other people.

It had been that way for a long time. Ever since that night that changed everything. The night that changed my family. That changed my relationship with Allie.

That was the night that I realized that even the people you love the most could let you down. It was the people you loved the most who would let you down beyond belief.

I learned that lesson the hard way, but it wasn't a lesson I would soon forget. The only people I trusted now, the only ones who I really let in, were Olly and Beck. They both knew about the problems in my family, but even they didn't know the full extent of it. The only ones who knew that truth were Allie and Lucas, and I wished more than anything that neither of them knew shit about me.

I wished that none of it had ever happened, but wishing wouldn't get me anywhere. I learned that a long time ago as well, because I had wished and wished and wished that my parents would change.

I wished that my father had never cheated on my mother, and I wished that I had never walked in on my mom after she found out.

That memory was nothing but a nightmare. I can still remember the way her face looked when her body was so limp, and I still hated her for it. I was far too young, and she was my fucking mother, but my father had been destroying her little by little over the years and it had finally become too much.

And nobody was there for me.

I didn't have my mom, I couldn't stand looking at my dad, and the girl I had been in love with let me down just like everyone else.

It had all felt like too much, and I hated even thinking about it.

I refused to think about it.

I climbed in my car and drove to the Clermonts' house without thought. I blasted music and rolled down my windows to stop my brain from thinking of things that were better left alone. But I knew that it was impossible.

If I was going to convince Allie to stay away from Eli, if I was going to convince her that she was better off spending time with me, I knew that I wasn't going to be able to bury everything I had felt for her anymore.

Allie was like an addiction. I didn't want her, I knew she was fucking poison for me, but every time I saw her, I could feel myself gravitating toward her more and more. It didn't matter that I hated her or had convinced myself I didn't want her. Just the sight of her or the smallest inhale of her scent made me feel crazy.

I wanted her even though she was bad for me.

I wanted her despite everything that had happened in our past.

And that only made me hate her more.

I climbed out of my car and didn't bother knocking as I walked inside. I knew Beck would leave the door open for me, and Mr. Clermont would die if I woke the whole house up in the middle of the night.

He was one of the nicest men I had ever met, but I still feared him enough not to test him.

As soon as I closed the door behind me, I could hear girly giggles coming from the living room. I smiled as I easily recognized Frankie's overzealous laugh.

"Shouldn't you all be in bed?" I rounded the corner, and the laughter died as soon as Allie's gaze met mine.

"Shouldn't you be off with some skank?"

I smiled because damn, these girls are protective.

Even though I'm still not quite sure how Josie feels about me, she makes it perfectly clear that when it comes to her friend, she will bury me before she lets me hurt her.

Fair enough.

But I don't have any real plans of hurting Allie. Not really. Not with anything more than the bullshit banter the two of us have every time we see each other. I never wanted Allie to be close enough to me again for me to hurt her or for her to hurt me.

But I was going to have to change that now.

I was going to have to convince her to get close to me. I was somehow going to convince her to fall for me.

And I knew that the simple solution would be for me to just tell Allie the truth. Fuck, actually, that was exactly what I needed to do.

Wasting my time and effort on convincing her to fall for me was futile. Because she would never fall for me. I may have had the slightest chance one upon a time, but not anymore.

Not after the way I've treated her.

I just needed to be honest with her.

"You know I don't bring the skanks home with me, Josie. They get too attached that way." I winked at Josie, and she rolled her eyes at my douchebag move. "But speaking of skanks…" I turned my attention to Allie. "I overheard a bunch of the guys talking tonight, and I should warn you. Eli is only interested in you because of some bet."

Her deep inhale was visible, and there was an instant look of defeat on her face. I told myself not to react. I didn't care that Allie was hurt by the news. She would have been far more hurt when he had done to her exactly what he had planned to do. I would much prefer that she find out now. That she find out from me.

"You are such an asshole." Her words were shaky, and

she forced herself to look away from me and down at her phone.

"I'm not sure how that makes me an asshole. I'm not the one who's using you." I shrugged my shoulders and made her believe I didn't care. I had become far too good at it.

"You seriously can't stand to see her be happy. Can you?" Frankie huffed and stood from the couch. There wasn't a trace of laughter or happiness left on her face that had been there when I walked in.

"This has nothing to do with me not wanting her happy. I figured she'd like to know now."

Frankie pushed her hand against my chest and forced me to take a few steps back and further and further away from Allie.

"Just like how that guy we saw at the pier last week wasn't really flirting with her."

"He wasn't." I chuckled even though thinking about that asshole made me feel ragey. "He was asking for directions."

"Right. And when Scott Noble asked for her number, but you convinced her that he just needed help with his homework."

"I don't really see your point."

She had pushed me so far back that we were now out of earshot of both Allie and Josie. It was just me and Frankie, and I hated that out of all of them she thought badly of me. She was pissed, and I knew Allie had become one of her best friends, but so had I.

"The point is that you are always telling Allie about how any guy who shows even the slightest bit of interest in her is after something else." She held up her hand and started counting on her fingers. "Schoolwork, sex, directions, her friend's number, and now, a bet. Come on, Carson. You're eventually going to have to get some balls and ask the girl out if you don't want her to be with someone else."

I shook my head and tried to ignore what she was saying. She had a point, but that wasn't what this was. I wasn't just bullshitting them. Eli was going to use her, and he was going to hurt her, and none of them believed me. "I don't care who she dates. I just think she should be prepared to be the laughingstock of both of our schools. If she still decides to trust the guy then that shit is on her."

She narrowed her eyes as she stared up at me. Frankie didn't believe a word I said. She had always been able to see right through me, and I hated that shit. "Are you sure that maybe you don't just want to be with Allie yourself, but you're too chicken to admit it?"

"Are you sure that you don't have feelings for Olly?" I stared down at her, and I hated that she flinched. I didn't want to hurt her, but I also wanted her to get off my back about Allie. "I see the way you look at him."

I could see her trying to come up with what to say. Frankie was always stuck in her head, and I had never called her out about Olly before. I didn't think anyone had. Olly would kill me if he knew. "How would you know what feelings look like, Carson? You never have feelings for anyone, right? And you definitely don't have any for Allie."

"You're right. I don't."

We stared at each other for a few moments without saying a word. I should have apologized for bringing up Olly. It was a low blow even for me. But Frankie spoke first.

"Stop being a dick to Allie."

I grinned down at her and gave her a grand salute with my hand.

"And don't bring up that other thing ever again. There's

no use talking about something that can never be." She looked so damn sad. So heartbroken by the thought that she could never be with Olly, and she was right. The two of them could never be together. Not if they wanted Olly to maintain his friendship with her brother.

Because as much as Beck loved us both like brothers, he would absolutely lose it.

"Don't worry, Frankie girl. Your secret is safe with me." I leaned forward and pressed a gentle kiss to her forehead, and I hoped it chased away some of the sadness that I had just caused.

She smiled at me, but it didn't come close to reaching her eyes.

"Good night, playboy."

"'Night." I didn't look back as I climbed the stairs to the Clermonts' spare bedroom. I didn't search the living room for another glance at Allie or tense as her laughter reached me once more.

And I sure as hell didn't dream about her that night or what I was going to have to do to convince the girl who hated me to fall for me.

Because she hadn't believed a single word I had said, which meant I was backed into a corner. I had no choice but to make Allie fall for me even though I had been convincing her to hate me for years.

CHAPTER 4
ALLIE

I kicked my feet through the pool water and tried to calm my racing thoughts. I had barely slept last night after Carson had come in and ruined my mood.

And what he said?

I couldn't stop thinking about it.

Was Eli just using me? Probably. But I didn't believe Carson about some dang bet or the fact that he thought he knew anything about the guy. He just didn't want to see me happy.

It was always the same. Any guy who was interested in me was always interested for some reason other than actually liking me, according to Carson. I knew that he was clearly still angry with me, that he had a deep-seated hate for me he couldn't let go of, but he was hurting me.

In the beginning, I tried to just let it roll off me, but his words refused to anymore. They struck me hard, and he always managed to hit me exactly where he was aiming. I guess that was part of the problem with making an enemy out of someone who used to know you so well. They knew exactly where to strike.

I could do the same to him if I wanted to. I knew where Carson hurt and where his weaknesses lied. Even if he tried to parade around like he was nothing but a careless playboy these days, I knew the truth. That wasn't who he was. Not really.

It was just some version of him that he had become.

Because Carson Hale was scared to get close enough to anyone who could possibly hurt him.

"There you are." I looked up just as Frankie and Josie walked out of the back sliding door. Frankie's house was massive, the pool to die for, and the view even better.

"Yeah." I ran my hand over my face and pushed back my soaking wet hair. "I couldn't sleep so I decided to go for a swim."

I smiled at them even though I knew they could see through it. The two of them were already in their bathing suits as well, and they each took a seat on either side of me.

"What's going on?" Josie nudged her shoulder into mine before laying her head on my shoulder. I pressed my head into hers and stared out over the view.

"Just stuck in my head."

"Do not let what Carson said last night get to you. You know he's always a dick to you for no reason. Eli wouldn't have asked you out if he didn't want to."

"No. I know." I nodded my head. "He actually already text me this morning."

"What?" Frankie leaned forward to get a good look at my face. "What did he say?"

"He said that he couldn't stop thinking about our dance last night and that he couldn't wait to see me again." I shrugged like it was no big deal, but the reality is that his text had made my heart race. Regardless of what Carson said, he had woken up this morning and thought of me.

"That's so cute." Frankie grinned. "What did you say back?"

"Nothing yet." I dragged my feet through the warm water, back and forth. "I didn't want to seem too eager."

"Good girl." Josie laughed before pressing a kiss to my cheek then sliding into the pool. "Make the boy work for it. No one deserves you if they aren't willing to put in some work."

"Do you..." I hesitated before taking a steadying breath. "Do you think he's really just using me like Carson said?"

"No." Josie's answer was firm. "Carson's just being an asshole. You know he always does this."

"I know." I looked back to the house because I knew Carson was still in there somewhere, and there was no way in hell I wanted him to hear me questioning everything because of a few simple words from him. "But Eli is on the baseball team, and we've never really interacted before. Maybe Carson is telling the truth."

"He's not." Frankie climbed into the water, too, before turning to face me. "Whatever Carson's problem is has nothing to do with these guys. It has to do with you. He's not like this with anyone else."

"I know." I groaned and ran my fingers down my face.

"What happened between you two? I know you don't really want to talk about it, but just give us something. It's hard for us to understand when we have no details."

I looked back to Frankie because I knew that she was close with Carson. She always defended me when he was being a jerk, but I knew she cared for him. It was hard not to when he didn't hate you.

"What has Carson told you?" I gripped the edge of the pool with my hands on either side of my thighs as I waited for her answer.

"He hasn't. He's as tight-lipped as you are about it."

"Come on, Allie." Josie moved in closer to us. "We're your best friends. We would never judge you or say anything about what happened. Did you two sleep together?"

"No." I laughed. I wished it had been as simple as that. "I don't know how much you all know about his parents." I looked back at the house again before continuing. "But they used to be so happy. When we were younger, Carson and I were close, and I would spend so much time at his house and him at mine."

"Okay?" Frankie encouraged me to go on.

"I used to be in love with him," I admitted out loud to them something that I didn't think I had ever said to anyone. "He was my best friend; he only cared about me as a friend, and I was in love with him."

"What happened?" Josie put her hand on my knee, and I didn't even realize that I was bouncing it until that moment.

"He was always interested in other girls. You know how he is. He can get any girl he wants. So, finally I decided that I was going to do the same. He didn't see me as anything other than his friend, and it literally killed me. This was years ago." I straightened and smiled and tried to play off how badly I had wanted him. "We were only fifteen at the time. He had just started hanging out with Lucas and the boys, and things were changing between us. I went out on a date, if you can even call it that, and he was so upset about it."

"Because he loved you too." Josie said it like it was so obvious, but she was wrong.

"No. He was just possessive. He didn't want me, but he didn't want anyone else to have me either. We got into a fight. The first one we had ever had because I went on the date. He blew my phone up while I was there, but I didn't answer. I didn't want him to ruin my chance with this guy who actually wanted me simply because Carson didn't want him to have me, you know?" I looked up to the sky and took a deep breath. "He wouldn't answer my calls or texts after. Wouldn't answer the door. I was so angry with him because I thought he was just punishing me. But I was so damn wrong. His mom had caught his dad cheating the night before."

Frankie's shocked inhale told me enough. They may have been friends, but Carson hadn't let them in. Not really.

"When Carson had gone home that night, he found his mother on her bathroom floor. She had overdosed on some pills she had in her cabinet and tried to kill herself, and he had been the one to find her. That was why he had been calling me. He was calling me because he needed me, and I wasn't there." I angrily wiped a tear from my face.

"You know that's not your fault, right?" Josie looked back and forth between me and Frankie. "There was nothing you could do."

"I know that." I nodded. "But I should have been there for him. I should have been happy with being his friend, not trying to make him jealous. Because that's all that date was. It was a ploy to try to get him to notice me as something other than his stupid friend, and I ruined everything."

"Allie."

I knew Josie was going to try to talk me off this ledge, that she was going to try to convince me that this was all on

Carson and his family, but she was wrong. If I had only answered my phone and been there for him, we wouldn't be where we are now.

He wouldn't still hate me.

"It doesn't matter." I shook my head and planted a fake smile on my face. "He never talked to me anymore after that. Not other than to insult me one way or another, and that's that." I shrugged my shoulders and both girls looked concerned.

"I didn't realize." Frankie looked up at the house then back at me. "I didn't know that about his parents. They are still together, and I didn't think what happened between the two of you would be this serious. I just thought he was pining after you."

"No." I laughed, just as the door opened behind me. "A girl could only wish."

I looked back over my shoulder to see Beck, Olly, and Carson walking outside. The three of them were talking, and I wasn't sure if they had even noticed us yet. I turned back to the water and quickly wiped at my face. There was no way I would allow him to catch me out here crying. It didn't matter if he didn't have a clue, it was over him.

I refused to give him any ammunition over me.

Frankie laughed and squeezed my leg just as I heard running behind me. Then Carson bolted past me, close enough that I could easily reach out and touch him, and jumped into the water. He managed to splash all three of us, but I was happy for the distraction.

I wiped the water from my face as he came back to the surface with a grin on his face. Don't look at him. Don't look at him.

"I didn't get you ladies wet, did I?" He grinned harder and Josie gagged audibly.

"I don't think you could get any douchier if you tried, Carson."

"Sure, I could." He swam toward her, and she held out her hands.

"I swear to God, Carson. Do not. Beck!" But Beck was too far away, and Carson had already gotten Josie's hand in his. He pulled her toward him, and she laughed as she tried to fight him off.

God, I hated him for who he had become, but when I watched him be like this with someone else, I also missed him. And I hated the deep ache in my stomach at the thought.

"Beck can't help you." He lifted Josie into the air, her body wiggling and trying to get out of his grip the entire time, before he tossed her in the air and to the deep end of the pool. "What are you two looking at?" He turned to me and Frankie. "Any comments you all would like to make this morning?"

"Nope." Frankie leaned against the back of the pool. "But it's not our fault you act like a prick before anyone has even had their coffee."

He dove for her before she even got the last few words out, and she squealed as he tried to grab ahold of her. "Say you're sorry, and I won't throw you."

"Not happening." Frankie laughed, and Carson caught ahold of her hand. His hand brushed my leg as they horse-played, and I tensed at the contact. I hadn't touched him in forever. His gaze met mine, as if he felt that brush as strongly as I had. It was only for a moment.

But it felt like a lifetime. I held my breath until he looked away from me. My stomach ached, my chest ached, and if I was being honest with myself, my thighs tightened from that one look alone.

"All right, Frankie girl. It was your choice." He lifted her in the air like he had Josie just moments before and threw her too.

I expected him to swim away, to not say another word to me since he didn't currently have anything to insult me about, but he didn't. He turned back in my direction, crossed his arms over his chest, and stared at me.

"What?" I asked consciously. I wished he would look anywhere but at me.

"You have anything that you'd like to say?"

"Absolutely not." I shook my head and gripped my fingers harder into the pool edge.

"You don't think I'll throw your ass into the pool too?" He cocked his head to the side, and I knew he was challenging me.

"I didn't think you even knew I existed when there wasn't another guy talking to me."

He jolted back as if my words shocked him, and I guess they probably did. I rarely ever said anything to him, let alone anything to defend myself in any way. Hell, before I became friends with Josie, I tried to avoid him at all costs.

"I think we both know that I'm well aware of the fact that you exist." He moved closer to me, and I straightened. What was he doing?

"Do we?" I looked behind him to where Olly was pulling Frankie to the shallow end of the pool. She was staring daggers at Carson's back, but he had no idea. His attention was all on me.

Nothing in this world scared me more.

The only time Carson paid me any attention was when he intended to hurt me, to berate me, to put me down. I couldn't handle any of those things right now. Not after the conversation I just had with the girls. The memories of who Carson and I used to be were still fresh in my mind, and I didn't want them tainted by this guy who stood in front of me now.

"Come on, Allie." He was less than a foot away from me. "Get in the water or I will drag your ass in."

"No." I shook my head and started to climb from the pool's edge, but he reached his hands out and grabbed ahold of my legs before I could. His hands held on to me just behind my knees, and I felt paralyzed by his touch.

"Carson, don't." My words were a whisper, only for me and him to hear, and I knew that he could hear the emotion in my voice that I had tried to hide.

"Why not?" His fingers tightened around my skin. "We're just having fun."

I looked down at him, and I couldn't help staring at his chest or the way it rose and fell with each of his breaths. His body was perfect, chiseled through athletics and years of surfing, and it felt so sinful to look at. There wasn't an innocent thought that ran through my mind as my gaze skimmed over his golden skin.

"You and I don't have fun anymore, remember?"

He chuckled and his stomach pressed into my shins. I couldn't remember the last time we had been this close, but it felt good. It felt so damn familiar. The warmth of his skin, the smell of his leftover cologne.

He was like the warmest of memories mixed with the harshest dose of reality.

Past and present. Then and now.

They were so different yet so familiar, and I couldn't keep my head on straight when the two of them became so clouded.

"I'm well aware, but honestly, I don't remember you being much fun back then either."

I knew he was trying to get a reaction out of me. That was what he wanted. "You're such a liar." I tried to pull out of his hold, but his grip was relentless.

"You're right." His truth shocked me. "Get in the water and remind me how fun you are."

"It's not happening. Let me go." His touch felt like a brand, burning me, consuming me, and I knew it wasn't meant to be. He was simply touching me, playing another one of his damn games, and I wasn't capable of having these stupid, insignificant moments with him. Every word, every look, every touch, it all meant too much.

"All right, Allie. Don't say I didn't warn you." He pushed between my thighs before he wrapped one of his arms around my back. He lifted me to him like I weighed nothing, and even though I didn't want to, I grabbed onto his shoulders to stop me from falling.

"Carson, put me down." My words were breathless in his ear. His hand tightened behind my back, his fingers relaxing before contracting again against my skin. My legs were wrapped around him, and I caught everyone watching us out of the corner of my eye.

"I'll make you a deal." Carson stopped in the center of the pool and looked straight into my eyes. "If you'll agree to go out on a date with me, I won't throw you."

"What?" I jolted backward, but his hands held me in place. "Have you lost your mind? Did you hit your head last night after we left the party?"

"No." He chuckled. "My head is perfectly clear."

"Is this a joke then? Are you trying to prove some point?" I squirmed in his arms and tried to put some space between us. "I'm not going to say yes, so you might as well go ahead and throw me."

"You wound me." He lifted me higher against him and readjusted his grip. I knew that I was about to be thrown into the water at any moment. "Can't a guy just be interested in his old friend?"

"Not you."

"I guess you would think that, huh?" He spun me in his arms until he was cradling me.

"Have you given me any reason to think differently? You hate me, Carson, and I don't think that fact has suddenly changed in the last few hours."

He stared down at my mouth before bringing his gaze back to meet mine. "I don't hate you."

Before I could take in his words or think of a response, he threw me. I flew through the air before hitting the water, and I let myself sink as the water surrounded me. I had no idea what the hell he was doing or why he was doing it, but I no longer trusted Carson Hale.

I knew that fact above all others.

But his words still shot through me like an assault. *I don't hate you.* They messed with my head and my heart, and I knew that was what he wanted.

I was nothing more than a game to him, and I refused to allow myself to get close enough for him to hurt me again.

CHAPTER 5

CARSON

I was pretty positive that Allie had been avoiding me since the pool. Not that I could blame her. I hadn't really been thinking clearly when I asked her out. I knew that I needed to get closer to her, and with any other girl, that wouldn't have been an issue. But Allie Taylor threw me off my game.

When I had touched her leg, I wasn't expecting it to be so damn soft and inviting. I wasn't expecting my stomach to tense up even though we weren't doing a thing. I had been with far too many girls for a simple touch of her leg to affect me.

But it still did.

Then every bit of my game went out the window, and I blurted out that she should agree to go on a date with me before I could think better of it.

She said no. Of course, she said no.

And the only thing I managed to do was make her guard go up a little bit more.

"What's your deal?" Olly threw me the baseball, and it hit my glove with a loud pop.

"I don't have a deal." I shrugged and threw the ball back. My arm was tired and my body wasn't happy with the amount of alcohol I drank this weekend, but I had a game to play so I would push through it. I always did. "What's your deal?"

"Don't act dumb." He threw the ball just the slightest bit harder this time. "What were you thinking asking Allie out?"

"Why?" I pulled the ball out of my glove and tossed it in the air. "Am I encroaching on your space? Were you going to ask her out?"

The thought alone made me irrationally angry. I caught the ball before throwing it back at Olly far too hard for someone who wasn't warmed up. He knew it too.

"No. Of course not." He shook his head. "You've already pissed all over her, and I wouldn't get between that little hate/love fest you both have going on if you paid me."

"You're so dramatic." I rolled my eyes at him. Beck was off to the side stretching, and I wished he was here as a buffer. I needed someone to help get Olly off my back or he wouldn't let this drop.

"Whatever you say. I just know that you've been making that girl's life a living hell for almost as long as I've known you, now you suddenly want to ask her out?"

"It was the cowgirl costume." I winked at him as I caught the ball again. "It's made me see the error of my ways."

"The same costume that you told her made her look like a slut?" He tilted his head to the side.

"Do you have an issue with me dating Allie?" I almost wished he would say yes.

I wished that he would convince me to stop because Olly was the most level-headed out of all of us. If he knew what I was doing, if he even had an inkling of an idea about the bet, he would kill me.

But I didn't have any other choice.

Not when the girls had blown off my warning like I had just told them it was going to rain. Eli was going to use her whether Allie wanted to admit it or not, and I couldn't just sit back and watch. I couldn't sit back and let Lucas and his boys think they could fuck with another girl who meant something to me.

Even though I had no idea what she meant anymore. If she meant anything at all. I just knew the thought made me want to kill every single one of them.

"Of course, I don't have an issue, but don't be a dick to her. Allie is a good girl. If you're just fucking with her, leave her alone."

"I didn't realize you were on her side on this." I pulled off my hat and flipped it around backward.

"I'm not on anyone's side. I just know you, and I don't think you have the best of intentions." He raised an eyebrow at me before throwing the ball again.

"I'm a saint."

He rolled his eyes and didn't even attempt to entertain me. "Just remember that she's Frankie's friend, and Frankie will kill you for hurting her."

"I haven't forgotten, but if you all can remember, I was friends with Allie long before any of you even knew who she was."

"Oh. We remember, and for whatever reason, you've taken it upon yourself to be cruel to her for years now. Why don't you just let her date Eli and get over it?" He nodded toward the dugout.

I turned in that direction and spotted Allie standing by

the fence instantly. She was talking to Eli, giggling at something he was saying, and I wanted to knock his teeth out.

She wouldn't normally be here at Prep after one of our practices so I knew either Frankie or Josie were somewhere close by.

I threw the baseball back to Olly without even looking before I headed in their direction. "I'm warm."

"We've barely even thrown."

I wasn't listening to him, though. I was headed straight for Eli and Allie, and I had no damn clue what I was going to say. He was mumbling to her as I approached. His hand above his head gripping the fence and his mouth far too close to her ear.

"Hey, Allie."

Her gaze snapped to mine, and she blushed as if she had just been caught doing something wrong. "Hi."

I stood directly next to Eli, my shoulder touching his, and I couldn't stop smiling when I heard his huff of frustration.

"Have you thought any more about my question?"

"I didn't realize you asked a question. It was more like a demand." She rolled her eyes, and her hands tightened on the fence.

"Well, let me do a better job then." I grinned at her. "Allie, would you like to have dinner with me tomorrow night?"

She looked away from me and down at her hands, and I knew that she was going to tell me no again. I expected it. But I wanted to make it clear in front of Eli that I was going after her. Whatever the fuck he thought he was trying to prove would fail.

"Sorry, bud," Eli answered before she had a chance.

"Allie and I just made plans for tomorrow. It looks like you're just a bit too late."

"You made plans with him?" I looked back and forth between them. Even after what I had told her.

"I did." She straightened her spine. "But that's not really your business, Carson. I don't have to suddenly run my plans by you."

God, she looked so gorgeous in the sunlight. Pure innocence. Her blonde hair was in loose waves down her back, and even though it was usually the first thing people noticed, it was her eyes that got to me. If you weren't looking close enough, you would think they were brown, but they weren't. They were the warmest shade of honey mixed with an emerald green.

"You're right. You don't." I shook my head and tried to stop taking in every little detail of her. I never let her see me like this. I needed to say something. I needed to figure out a way to stop her from going out with him. "Where are you all going? If you've decided to pick Eli over me, then we can make a double date out of it."

"That's not..."

She was cut off by Eli saying, "Wings and Things."

"Fancy." I wagged my eyebrows at her, and she tried to hide her smile but couldn't. "What time should I meet you?"

"I don't think this is a very good idea." Allie took a step back from the fence and looked over her shoulder to where I knew her friends were waiting for her. Frankie waved when she saw me looking, and I nodded.

"It's a great idea." I put my arm around Eli's shoulders. He tensed, his whole body going rigid beneath my arm. "Me, you, your new man. I'll make sure to bring a date that you'll like. We'll have the best time. Right, Eli?"

He looked up at me, and he wasn't nearly as cocky without Lucas by his side. "If that's what Allie wants."

"It's not." She laughed and looked up to the sky with her hands on her hips. "But I know you're not going to leave this alone unless I agree."

"Exactly." I clapped Eli on the shoulder then started walking into the dugout. "So, I'll see the two of you at six?"

Because there was no way in hell I was letting her go out with him on her own. Even if I had to sit there and watch Eli try to flirt with her. Even if she smiled at him like she had been when I walked up.

I would suffer through it all, and when she realized that Eli was nothing but an asshole, we would go back to exactly what we were before.

CHAPTER 6
ALLIE

If I wasn't already nervous when I agreed to go on a date with Eli, I definitely was now. I had no idea what the hell Carson was doing or thinking, but I knew that whatever it was, it wasn't something that would be good for me.

Because Carson didn't care about me.

I didn't know if Eli had stirred some competitive instinct in him or if he simply didn't want to see me happy with someone he knew, but I knew that tonight would be a disaster before I even started getting ready.

Every little decision I made was meticulously thought over: the way I wore my hair, my makeup, the length of my jean shorts. I didn't want to give Carson anything to use against me, and I knew he would if he got the chance. He always did.

I walked into Wings and Things and spotted Eli as soon as I made it through the door. He smiled before standing and coming to meet me. I couldn't tell if anyone else was already at the table, and I tried to remind myself that I shouldn't care. Tonight was about having fun and getting to know Eli.

Carson didn't matter for either of those things. I would just drown him out and pretend he wasn't there. That was what I was used to doing. That was what the two of us had been doing for years.

Even though I was already a little but irritated that Eli hadn't offered to pick me up. My dad was irritated by that fact too.

"You look beautiful." Eli grinned before pulling me into a hug.

"Thank you." I breathed in the scent of his warm cologne, the smell familiar and calming. "You look nice as well."

I looked up at him as he let me go. He was much taller than me, although shorter than Carson, and he had a smile that made me feel comfortable.

He grabbed my hand in his and led the way back to the table. I fixed my hair while I was still blocked from view, and I planted the best smile I could manage on my face as he pulled out the chair for me that was directly across from Carson.

"Thank you." I settled into my seat and tried to avoid making eye contact with Carson.

"Allie, this is Kimberly. Kimberly, Allie. I think you all might know each other."

I looked across the table at Kimberly, and of course I knew her. We had gone to school together since grade school, and I had hated her almost as long. She was popular, conceited, and a perfect fit for Carson.

"Of course." I nodded and pulled out my menu. "How are you, Kim?"

"I'm perfect." She giggled and looked over at Carson. His hand disappeared under the table, and even though I couldn't see it, I knew that his hand probably rested on her thigh.

I wanted to rip it off.

"Awesome," I mumbled and tried to focus on the menu.

Carson laughed under his breath, but I ignored him.

"What are you getting?" I looked to my right where Eli sat. "Do you want to share some wings?"

"Oh." He looked up from his menu. "I was thinking about getting the burger."

"A burger at a wing place." Carson scoffed and tossed his menu down on the table. "I'll share an order with you, Allie. Kim's getting a salad."

He didn't give me time to answer. As soon as the waitress came to our table, Carson opened his mouth. "My girl Allie and I are going to share a large order of wings, extra ranch for both of us. No carrots. She hates those."

I looked at him like he had lost his mind because I was pretty sure that he had.

"What can I get you to drink?" The waitress was now looking at me.

"Um, just a Coke, please."

Everyone else ordered their food, and I fidgeted with my hands under the table.

"So, Allie, how is school going for you?" I looked up at Eli. I had almost forgotten he was there.

"It's all right. I'm so ready for fall break, though."

"Me too." He nodded. "Are you going anywhere? My family is taking a trip to Europe."

"No." I almost choked on the word. Sometimes I forgot just how far apart my family was from those who went to

Prep. They were made of money, old money to be exact, and guys like Eli had never had to think about working or how he'd pay for college. "We typically stay home and do a Thanksgiving meal at our house. It's real low-key."

And my dad would still be working every day except for Thanksgiving, and my small house would be busting with people. My grandparents, aunts, uncles, cousins. We were always together on holidays, and I loved it.

It may not have been Europe, but it was ours.

"That's cool." He nodded and turned his chair to where he faced me better. "We've been going to Europe for years now. My parents love it, and they take us about every other year. Have you ever been?"

"To Europe?" I shook my head, and suddenly I felt ridiculous. "No. The farthest I've been is Disney World." I didn't mention that had been almost ten years ago.

I could hear Carson and Kimberly talking across from us, and I hoped he was too enthralled with her and her perfect face to even consider listening to our conversation.

Eli laughed like I had just told a joke, but I hadn't. "That's too bad. I bet you would really like Europe."

"What makes you think that, Eli?" Carson was leaned back in his chair with his arm resting on the back of Kimberly's.

Eli laughed nervously and looked between me and Carson. "It's Europe." He shrugged his shoulders.

"But you don't know anything about Allie specifically that would make her love Europe, correct?"

Eli opened his mouth, but Carson continued.

"Like you have no clue that she's been dreaming of going to Paris forever, and she has this little Eiffel Tower key chain that she's had on her set of keys since she's had them. Or that she thinks she's part Irish because she has a little bit of green in her eyes."

"I didn't realize you knew so much about her." Eli was no longer aloof. He was sizing Carson up, and I wasn't here for a pissing contest.

"Well, now you do." Carson stared back at him with the same unrelenting gaze, and I felt like I was going insane.

Carson hadn't given a shit about me since that night he needed me and I wasn't there. If he wasn't ignoring me altogether, he was making me wish he was, and now all of the sudden, he wanted to share wings and spew facts about me like he was my best friend.

"Stop," I hissed. "You're being an ass. Aren't you supposed to be on your own date?" I looked over at Kimberly, and she looked uncomfortable. I couldn't blame her. I felt uncomfortable too.

The waitress arrived back at our table with food in hand, and we were spared from whatever Carson was going to say next. He looked down at the food, and his bright eyes looked so hollow. He scrunched his brow, something he always did when he was upset, and his jaw stiffened. I didn't know if he was angry with me or with himself.

But I didn't want to find out. I quickly grabbed a wing from our plate and took a huge bite. Sauce dripped down my chin, but I didn't stop. The food was a distraction. If we were eating, then we weren't talking, and I couldn't stand to hear anything more from Carson right now.

Not after everything he just said. Not with the way he had brought up memories of me like it wouldn't mess with my head.

"This is good." I wiped at my mouth with the back of my

hand. "Do you want a bite?" I looked over to Eli, and he shook his head as he looked at my half-bitten wing.

"Nah. I'm good."

"Suit yourself." I shrugged as I looked down at his measly-looking burger.

"I'll take one." Carson reached forward, his fingers wrapping around my wrist, and he stood in his seat enough to bring my hand to his lips. I stared at him, shocked by what he was doing, but there wasn't an ounce of shame in his gaze.

He didn't look away from me for a second as he bit down into the wing I was still holding, and I couldn't stop myself from holding my breath as his lips met my fingers. Carson Hale wasn't just taking a bite of my chicken. He was causing a scene, and part of me wondered how he had gotten so damn good at it.

He ran his tongue over the edge of my thumb, licking up the sauce that had dripped there, and I felt like he had just used his tongue on parts of my body that no one else ever had. I pressed my thighs together as I watched his mouth, and I couldn't bring myself to care that Eli was watching me as Carson finally let go of my hand and settled back into his seat.

"You're right, Allie. That's absolutely delicious." He licked his lip before picking up a wing of his own, then began eating like that display hadn't just happened.

I picked up my napkin, quickly dropping my gaze to my lap as I wiped my hands, but I couldn't get the feel of him off. And I didn't know if I wanted to.

We ate the rest of our food in awkward silence. Eli barely spoke two words after that, and I honestly just wanted to leave. As far as first dates went, I would rate this one zero out of ten, but I knew that wasn't Eli's fault. He didn't have a fair chance. Carson refused to allow him to have one, but I still found myself not very interested in going out with him again.

Maybe that was Carson's plan all along.

I quickly text Frankie and Josie as Eli and Carson paid. They argued over that too. Carson insisted on paying for my food since we had shared, and Eli insisted on at least paying for my drink.

I just wanted to pay for my own meal, climb in my car, and pretend this entire night had never happened.

"Thank you for tonight," I told Eli as we walked next to my car. Carson was just a couple of cars over talking to Kimberly, and I wanted to get out of here before he got a chance to do or say anything else.

"You're welcome." He tucked his hands into his front pockets and rocked onto his heels as he looked over his shoulder. "I'm sorry it was such an odd date. I really hadn't planned on having a couple of date crashers."

"It's fine." I tried to laugh it off.

He took a small step toward me, and his body blocked my view of Carson. "The next date is just you and me, deal?"

"Deal," I agreed quickly, too quickly, and found myself questioning my decision.

"I'll text you tonight then." He leaned forward, and I tensed as his mouth moved toward mine. I was into Eli. He was handsome and popular, and he was everything a girl should want. But it felt wrong.

This wasn't the right moment for a first kiss, and I found myself dreading it the closer and closer he got to me.

He got so close to me that his body crowded mine, and if I leaned up on my tiptoes, our lips would have easily met.

But I didn't do that. Instead, I turned my head to the side just as he closed the gap between us, and his lips met my cheek.

He stood there for a moment, clearly shocked that I turned away from him, before he pulled back with a cocky grin on his face. "'Night, beautiful."

"Good night."

He stepped back before he ran his hand through his hair, and I quickly climbed into my car. I took a deep breath as I started the engine. I quickly checked my phone and saw about a hundred laughing emojis from Frankie and an eye roll from Josie.

I had text them to let them know that their friend was ruining my date. A date that they both agreed he shouldn't have even been on. Frankie thought the whole situation was kind of funny, but Josie had wanted to pummel Carson when I told her.

In hindsight, I should have let her. If I had, my fingers wouldn't still be tingling from where his mouth had touched them, and I wouldn't be looking in my rearview mirror for a glimpse of him instead of my date.

There was a loud knock at my window, and I jumped. My phone flew from my hand and onto the floorboard, and I scrambled to find it just as Carson pulled open my door.

"What are you doing?"

"That date was a bore." He leaned into my car, and I could see him scanning over every surface. It made me feel inadequate. My car was an old hand-me-down that my mother used to drive, and his was some sports car I didn't know the name of but probably cost as much as my house. "Let's do something fun."

"I'm not doing anything with you." I looked at him like

he was insane. "I'm going home and finishing a paper that's due next week."

He shook his head and leaned further into my car. For a moment I thought he was going to kiss me, but he simply turned off my car and jerked my keys out of the ignition before I could stop him.

"What are you doing?" I tried to snatch my keys out of his hand, but it was no use.

"I told you." He tucked my keys into his pocket and backed away from my car. "Having fun."

I told myself that I had no choice but to follow him. He had my keys. Unless I wanted to call one of my friends and explain that I had just let Carson reach into the car I was sitting in and take my keys from me.

So against my better judgment, I climbed out of my car, and I followed my ex-best friend.

CHAPTER 7
CARSON

I was shocked as hell when Allie didn't immediately yell at me and started following me to my car. I was even more shocked when I opened the passenger door with a cocky smile on my face and she climbed in without an argument.

"Where exactly are we going?" She held her purse in her lap, and she was staring out of the window as I backed out of the parking spot.

"You need to live a little." I looked over, distracted by the way she bounced her knee. She was in a pair of tiny blue jean shorts, and her legs were on full display. I knew that she hadn't done that for me. It was for her date, but my cock didn't care.

Her skin was so smooth and begging to be touched, and I had ruined any chance of that happening for her tonight. When I had invited myself on their date, I hadn't exactly planned everything through.

Cock-blocking was really my one and only goal, but Eli was such a tool. He didn't know shit about Allie, and even worse, he didn't care to. But she had still been smiling at him like it was the greatest date she had ever been on, and she deserved more than that.

God, I hoped she realized that.

I couldn't stand the idea that she thought this was what she could possibly want.

"I live plenty, thank you."

"Do you?" I ran my hand through my hair and relaxed into my seat. "I bet you haven't been surfing in years or roller skating." Those used to be two of her favorite things in the world once upon a time.

"Of course not, Carson. I'm not a kid anymore. I have school and work and picking up extra shifts. College will be here before we know it, and I have to be ready to pay for my tuition." She huffed and toyed with a piece of her hair.

I knew what she was thinking. I didn't have to do those things. Not besides school, and even then, I could make shit grades and I would still be able to afford college. Allie always thought that was the biggest difference between me and her. Our families' money. But she was wrong.

Her family may not have had the old money that mine did, but they had everything else that we were lacking. At least they did when I still knew them.

"Okay. Then let's make a bet."

"What kind of bet?"

"For tonight, just for tonight, you have to say yes to everything I want us to do."

"Oh, is that all?" She chuckled and rolled her eyes. "Then what exactly is in this for me?"

"Well." I thought about what Allie could possibly want from me, and there was only one thing. "After tonight, I will leave you alone. No more cock-blocking you and Eli. No more asshole comments."

She turned in her seat, her knee pushing onto the console, and she gaped at me. "Just like that?"

"Just like that. Simple, easy."

"I only have to agree to five things that you say tonight."

"Twenty," I blurted, and she laughed.

"There's no way in hell. Ten."

"Deal." I stuck out my hand, and she hesitantly took it in hers.

"So, what's first? It's already eight-thirty."

"Calm down. You're not going to turn into a pumpkin at midnight, and I'm sure your mom won't care what time you come home if you tell her you're with me."

"I swear, your ego never ceases to amaze me. My mom might have felt like that once, but not anymore."

She was lying. I had seen Mrs. Taylor out at the gas station just a few weeks ago, and she wouldn't stop telling me about how much she missed me around her house. I wasn't sure how much Allie had told her about what happened between us or where our relationship stood now, but if she knew, she wasn't fazed by it.

"Give me your phone."

"What? No."

"This is yes number one, Allie. Give me your phone."

She grumbled before sliding her phone out of her back pocket and into my hands. I quickly found her contacts and clicked on Mom. It rang for a few seconds before Mrs. Taylor answered.

I pressed speaker and set her phone in my lap.

"Well, how was it? Was he a total gentleman or did you get a first kiss?"

"Oh my God," Allie grumbled and covered her face, and I couldn't help but laugh.

"Hi, Mrs. Taylor. This is actually Carson."

"Oh." She chuckled. "I didn't realize Allie was with you. I thought she was out on a date."

"She was." I nodded even though her mom couldn't see me. "But it was a bit of a bust, if you ask me."

"Nobody did," Allie whispered, and I quickly reached out and covered her mouth. Allie tried to tug my hand away, but I didn't budge.

"Well, that stinks. I had high hopes for this guy."

"It's okay. I'm going to take her out to have the best night of her life if you're okay with that. She said she had a curfew, but I was hoping just for tonight."

Allie licked the palm of my hand like she thought that was going to make me move my hand, but she was absolutely wrong. It did nothing but make my dick stir in my pants.

"Oh!" I could practically hear the smile in her voice. "Yes. You two go and have fun! If that's what Allie wants to do, she rarely ever does anything fun these days."

"That's exactly what I said." I slowly pulled my hand away from her mouth, and I let my fingers brush over her lips. I shouldn't have, but I couldn't help it. "I'll let you talk to her, though. Here she is."

I handed the phone to Allie, and she rolled her eyes. "Hey, Mom."

She was already trying to take the phone off speakerphone when her mom started talking. "Allie girl, I call that a trade-up. Eli Scott doesn't hold a candle to Carson Hale."

"Oh my God, Mom." Allie shoved the phone against her ear and looked so damn adorable when she was embarrassed. "Yes. He heard you. I can just come home if you want me to."

I had no idea what her mom said on the other line, but Allie pushed her head back against the headrest and looked so frustrated.

"Yes."

"Okay."

"I will be home before then. I have school tomorrow."

"I love you too. Bye."

Allie tucked her phone back in her pocket as I laughed. "I told you that your mom loves me."

"My mom has a bad judge of character when it comes to boys."

"Not true." I turned into my neighborhood. "Your dad is awesome."

"Well, yeah." She looked around. "He's the one exception. Where are we going?"

"My house." I nodded ahead at my giant home that looked so cold. "Yes number two is going surfing."

"No." She shook her head as I pulled into the driveway. "It'll be dark soon, and I don't have my swimsuit."

I parked my car and turned off the ignition. "Just go in your bra and panties."

"That's not happening." She was still shaking her head as I climbed out of the car and made my way to her side.

I opened her door and leaned inside. "Come on. You can wear one of my t-shirts then."

"And a pair of shorts." She crossed her arms, and I knew she wouldn't get out until I agreed. I may not have known much about Allie anymore, but I knew how stubborn she was. She always had been.

"Fine. You do realize I saw you in a bikini like two days ago, though, right?"

"It doesn't matter."

"Fine." I chuckled at how ridiculous she was being and held up my hands. "You can wear a pair of my sweats if you think you can surf in them."

Allie climbed out of my car, seeming satisfied with my answer, and I took a deep breath of her scent as she pushed past me. I didn't know what I was thinking. Allie brought up too many memories. She was the past, and that's where I should have kept her. Even the smell of her felt far too much like coming home.

A home I hadn't had in a very long time.

I closed the passenger side door and forced myself to snap out of it. Everything I was doing with her right now was for a reason. None of it mattered, not really, and none of it was real.

I either let Eli use her for their damn bet and mind my business, or I had to man the fuck up and remember what I was doing. Allie wasn't my friend, and she sure as hell wasn't anything more. It didn't matter what I felt or how my body reacted to her.

I wouldn't fall into this girl's trap again.

I had been in love with her once, far too obsessed with her than I was even willing to admit, and I had hated her after everything that happened with my parents. And part of me knew that Allie had nothing to do with it.

But another part of me, the part that I clung to, knew that Allie had been moving on from me and our friendship long before that night. She had been the only damn thing I cared about, and she was off on a date with someone else.

It wasn't fair to her that I was so angry that she was on a

date. I had been dating other people too. But that was her choice. I would have been hers if she wanted me. Those other girls had been nothing but a distraction from her.

Because Lucas told me that I looked like a desperate puppy chasing her around all day. I knew he was right, but God, that hurt back then. I was such a damn pussy, and she could have cared less that I was even there.

She hadn't answered when I called, when I needed her. She ignored me, and I knew that I was far too attached to her.

I told myself that day that I wouldn't be that way again. I was a teenager, and I was supposed to be having the time of my life. I didn't have time to chase after girls who had no real interest in me, and I definitely didn't have time to get my heart broken by them.

"I haven't been here in forever." Allie stared up at my house as we walked toward the door.

She hadn't been here since before everything happened with my parents.

"It's still the same." I shrugged off her comment and opened the front door.

She stepped inside and wrung her fingers together while she waited for me. "It does look the same." She laughed as she looked around. "I don't know why, but I was expecting it to look completely different."

Because we're different.

"Come on." I waved toward the hallway that led to my room. "Let's get some clothes before my parents realize we're here."

She didn't say a word. She just followed behind me and stepped inside my room just before I closed the door.

"Now, this looks different." She moved in a circle around

my room, and I watched her. We used to spend so much time in here and in her room, and once upon a time, her being here had felt like the most natural thing.

Now, I felt like I was holding my breath as she took in all of my things.

"I've grown up a bit since the last time you were in here."

"Have you, though?" She bent down and grabbed a comic book from the ground beside my bed. "It doesn't seem like you've grown up too much."

"That's probably been down there for years."

She rolled her eyes. "Oh, yes, because I'm sure it's been that long since your housekeeper has vacuumed." She sat down on the edge of my bed and flipped through the comic like it was the most natural thing in the world.

And God, she looked so good. Her long legs were begging me to spread them apart, and what I wouldn't give to bury my face between them. I would die to have her squirming beneath me and calling out my name.

I pushed off the doorframe and made my way to my dresser before I got any other stupid ideas. I pulled out my swimming trunks before tossing a pair on the bed beside her. Then I fumbled through my t-shirts until I found one that wouldn't swallow her whole.

"You can change in the bathroom" —I pointed toward my bathroom even though she knew exactly where it was— "and I'll change out here."

"Okay." She laid down the comic on my bedside table and scooped the clothes off my bed. She didn't look at me as she closed the bathroom door behind her, and I prayed she didn't hear my head thump against the wall as I tried to get my head on straight.

I shouldn't have brought her here. I should have just gone, hell, I don't know, but somewhere else. Anywhere else.

I changed into my shorts, tossing my shirt and jeans into the corner of my room, and sat on the edge of the bed as I waited for her. A snort left my mouth before I could stop it when she finally emerged.

"You look insane." She held her clothes in her arms, but it was the way my t-shirt hung to her mid-thigh and my shorts were almost to her ankles that had me laughing.

She tugged at my shorts with one hand, holding them up, and shrugged. "They're a little big."

"You think?" I climbed off the bed. "Just take off the shorts."

"Not in your house," she whispered as if I had just suggested that the two of us fuck on the kitchen counter. "I'll take them off on the beach, but I'm not running into your parents without pants on."

"Fine." I laughed. There was a very slim chance that we would see either of my parents. If they were home, they were usually nowhere to be seen. "Let's go."

We walked through my house and out to the garage. I grabbed my surfboard from the rack that lined the wall, then grabbed my old board from behind it and handed it to her.

"I can't believe you still have this thing." She ran her hand over the deck where both of our names were engraved into the polished wood.

"I don't think I could ever get rid of that thing." I stared at our names before looking back up at her. "It's seen too much."

"That it has." She followed me out of the garage and into the sand.

My house sat right on the beach, and it was the one and

only thing I loved about it. I used to escape out our garage door and into the ocean every time my parents would start fighting. I already had a love for surfing before then, but it became a lifeline.

We made our way down to the ocean, Allie trailing behind me as she struggled to keep my shorts up, and I let my feet hit the water before I stopped.

"Okay. Don't look. I have to get these dang shorts off," she huffed in frustration.

"I'm not looking," I lied as I watched her bend down and step out of my shorts. There was still nothing to be seen. Her body was completely covered by my t-shirt, with the exception of her legs.

She stood, her gaze meeting mine, and I smiled. Her cheeks became reddened so quickly, but she simply rolled her eyes. She stepped out into the ocean with my board at her side, and I followed her in.

Neither one of us spoke as we climbed onto our boards and paddled out into the ocean. The waves were relatively calm today, and I could only see a few other people down the beach from where we were.

Allie sat up on her board, letting her legs hang over the sides into the water, and leaned her head back to soak in the last moments of the slowly sinking sun. "I haven't done this in forever."

"What, come out here so late in the evening?" The sun was still bright enough that we could clearly see what we were doing, but it would be gone soon enough.

"No." She shook her head and trailed her fingers through the water. "Surfed. Been out here on a board."

"How long has it been?" I couldn't imagine going more than a couple days without being out here.

"When was the last time you and I talked? I'd say a few days before that."

I looked at her like she had lost her mind. "You haven't been surfing since the last time you went with me?"

"No." She shook her head and finally looked at me. "I haven't wanted to."

She used to. I wanted to remind her of that, and I wanted to demand she tell me why she hadn't since then. I wanted her to admit something that I wasn't even sure I was looking for.

Instead, the only thing I said was, "You might have lost your touch."

"Maybe." She chuckled. "But I didn't have much of a touch to start with. You just tried to make me think I was better than I actually was."

She was right, but I wasn't admitting that.

I paddled in the water, turning my board as a wave started to build. "Well, let's see what you got."

She eyed the same wave and quickly got into the right position on her stomach without me saying a word. She looked so determined as the wave made its way toward us.

The ocean pushed us both forward, and I was so damn distracted watching her that I could barely pay attention to what I was doing.

She stood on her board, something I had taught her years ago, and she rode the wave for a second or two before she wiped out and hit the water. I rode the wave out before jumping off my board and grabbing both boards in my hands.

Allie was now standing, wiping the water from her face, and my t-shirt was stuck to her like a second skin. It did nothing to hide her body which had become so damn perfect.

Her breast looked like they would fit in my hands perfectly, and God, I knew her strong thighs could hold her against me while I did whatever I wanted with her body.

"Quit looking at me like that." She pushed her curls out of her face and reached out for her board.

"Like what?" I was still staring at her, at the soft curve of her stomach and the deeper curve of her hips.

"Like that." She pointed at me and moved back out toward the deeper water.

"You going again?"

"I am." She climbed onto the board. "That was just pathetic."

"You're out of practice." Be an ass. Push her away. "It would seem you've been riding too many other things besides a board lately."

Her gaze snapped to mine, and I tried to ignore the hurt in her face as I pushed myself onto my own board.

"You're such an ass, Carson. I almost forgot that for a second there." She shook her head.

"Don't."

"I won't." She looked back at me over her shoulder, and I felt like she wanted to say something more. And part of me wished she would. I wished that the two of us could just have it out and quit tiptoeing over our past. "You won't let me."

CHAPTER 8
ALLIE

I was still shivering when I climbed into his car.

We had surfed without saying another word to each other for about half an hour until the sun was too low for us to continue. I didn't want to get out of the water when Carson said it was time to go. I just wanted to keep going, to keep pushing my body to do better, and to keep staring daggers at Carson and his perfect form.

I had actually been having fun there for a second until he had to go and ruin it.

I was disappointed when he had, but I expected it. That was all Carson did anymore when it came to me.

I didn't even understand why I was sitting here in his stupid fancy car with my hair still wet and my bra still damp against my skin. I had dressed in his room quickly then walked out before he was finished. I didn't want to do anything else with him today. I didn't want to say yes to the stupid little game he was playing.

I wanted to go home and snuggle into my bed and pretend like this entire night hadn't happened.

The sound of his car door opening startled me. I straightened in my seat as he climbed in and started the ignition, and I tried to pretend like the smell of his cologne didn't do something to me. His entire car smelled like it, but there was something different about smelling it on him.

"Where to now?" He looked over at me, and I wanted to slap that damn smirk from his face.

"I want to go home."

"What?" He frowned and looked back out the windshield. "No way. You've only said yes to two things so far. You owe me eight more."

"I don't owe you anything," I corrected him. "It's not going to stop you from being a dick anyway. Just take me home."

He ran his hand through his sandy blond hair before turning his head to look at me. He watched me for a moment before he even uttered a word. "I'm sorry, okay? I shouldn't have said that."

"I think you owe me more apologies than just that one."

I regretted the words as soon as I said them.

"That's probably true, but I don't think either one of us is ready for that conversation. Just give me tonight. I swear. No more asshole comments." His fingers drummed against the steering wheel, and even though I knew that I shouldn't, I trusted what he said.

I leaned my head back against the headrest and stared up at the ceiling. "I should say no."

"But you don't want to."

He was staring over at me, and I turned to look at him. He didn't look like the guy he tried to make everyone else believe he was. He looked like my Carson, like my old friend.

"No. I don't."

He grinned before he seemed to catch himself and what he was doing. That he let his guard down in front of me. "Let's go on our next adventure then."

"That word coming out of your mouth makes me nervous."

He chuckled as he backed out of the driveway. I noticed both of his parents' cars were here, but I didn't see either one of them. It was odd. "It's almost ten o'clock on a weeknight. How much trouble do you think we can get into?"

"With you?" I stared out the windshield and tried not to look at him again. I would never get my head on straight if I kept staring at his jawline or the short stubble of hair that rested there. "Probably too much."

He grinned but didn't say another word. He just drove, me having no idea where we were going, and I leaned back and just tried to enjoy it. Normally, I would be just getting off work or finishing up my homework, and even though there was no way I would admit it to him, it was nice to not have any obligations tonight.

My phone vibrated in my pocket, and I quickly checked it.

I hope you have a great night.

Guilt overwhelmed me as I read Eli's text, and I wasn't sure if it was because I felt guilt toward him or if I felt guilt toward Carson. Either way, I didn't respond to his message. I simply tucked my phone into my pocket and looked up just as Carson pulled into Bob's Snow Cones.

It used to be our favorite place ever.

I bounced in my seat, but then noticed the almost empty parking lot and the closed sign hanging from the building.

"They're closed." I pointed out the obvious to Carson, but he was already climbing out of the car.

He leaned back in, his arm resting on the hood of the car. "Come on or we'll miss the snow cones."

He shut the door, and I climbed out, following closely behind him as he walked to the side of the building. The door was cracked open, and I could see the smallest trail of light coming out from inside.

"I don't think we're supposed to just walk in when the place is closed, Carson."

He looked back at me before shaking his head with a smile. "You've gotten really boring with old age."

"I am not boring." I crossed my arms but still followed him. "I'm just responsible."

"Uh-huh." He rapped his knuckles against the old metal door that had too many dents and dings to count, then leaned against the building as he watched me.

It was only a moment later when Bob, the owner who was always here, opened the door and stuck his head outside. He looked exactly the same as he always had. His dark brown hair was brushed back out of his face, and his overgrown beard was as wild and carefree as his smile.

"Well, I'll be damned." He chuckled and opened the door wider. "I haven't seen the two of you together in... I can't remember when."

Carson took the door from his hand and followed him inside the small building.

"Allie, how have you been? I haven't seen you in forever." Bob pulled me into a hug as soon as I made my way through the door, and he smelled so sweet.

I hugged him back, a bit awkwardly, before stepping back and almost running into a box. "I've been good. Just busy with school and work."

He nodded with the most genuine smile on his face

before hiking his thumb over his shoulder at Carson. "I bet this one is the one who ran you off. Huh?"

"I didn't run anyone off."

"He did."

Carson and I answered at the same time causing Bob to laugh. It was deep and pure, and I missed the sound. I hadn't realized it until that moment.

I rarely came here anymore because I used to only come here with Carson, and I guess subconsciously, I had been avoiding any place the two of us went together.

"Well, have a seat and let me get you both a cone." Bob waved to the counter where Carson had already hopped onto.

I made my way over and hesitantly climbed onto the counter next to Carson. "You still come here a lot?"

"Uh, yeah," he said it like there wasn't any other option. "I'm taking it that you don't."

"Obviously not."

"Allie, you still a cherry girl?" Bob called out over the shaved ice machine.

"I am." I grinned. I couldn't believe he still remembered that.

"So plain." Carson leaned back against the wall and checked his phone.

"I happen to love cherry. Thank you very much."

"That's fine, but sometimes you just need to try new things. How do you know you prefer cherry over raspberry bombshell if you've never tried it?" He typed on his phone before tucking it back in his pocket, and I was dying to know who he was talking to.

Was it one of his girls? One of the girls he always had on his arm but never stuck around for long?

"I just know. Some of us don't have to taste every dang flavor there is before we realize what we want." I huffed. We were talking about snow cones flavors, and he was still getting to me.

That damn smirk that rarely left his face was back again, and he leaned forward until he was far too close to me. The small building echoed with the sound of Bob making our snow cones, and the bright lights should have done something to snap me out of my thoughts.

But all I seemed to hear was my heart racing and the sound of his breath mingling with mine. He was so close, and his gaze moved to my mouth. He watched me so intently, like he was trying to memorize my every move, and I couldn't pretend like it didn't affect me.

"I haven't tasted all of the flavors, you know." He didn't pull his gaze away from my mouth as he spoke, and some crazy part of me thought that he wanted to kiss me.

There was only the smallest amount of space separating us, and it would take only one of us giving in and leaning forward the tiniest amount for it to happen. It would take nothing and everything at the same time.

Because I knew if Carson kissed me, I would never be the same.

It would mean nothing to him and everything to me, and I would be wrecked after. I couldn't survive Carson twice. I was barely still surviving from the first time.

But even knowing that, I still desperately wanted him to kiss me. His breath brushed against my lips and my fingers ached against the counter as I tried to force myself to hold still.

I tried to force myself to remember exactly who he was.

"You mean to tell me there are a few girls in this town that you've missed?"

He chuckled, his gaze finally meeting mine. "One or two."

"You're such a pig, Carson." Neither one of us moved away, though. He was still so close and so overwhelming, and I knew that I should have put space between us. I should have demanded that he back away. But I did neither of those things.

"I'm well aware, but you still agreed to come out with me tonight."

"Agreed is really pushing it." I looked down at his hand as it inched closer to mine before looking back up at him. He was so sure of himself, of this, and I knew that Carson was far more experienced than I was. He flaunted that in my face almost every day. But I didn't know how to do this.

If I was being honest, I wished I could have been the kind of girl that could bring him to his knees. I wished that I could make him beg for everything I had and everything I could give him, but I knew it would likely be the other way around.

If I wasn't careful, I would easily beg him for everything we once had.

"You wanted to come." He lifted his hand, bringing it to my chest, and twisted one of my curls around his finger. "Allie Taylor doesn't do anything she doesn't want to do."

"You have no idea what I want." I swallowed and prayed he didn't notice how nervous he made me.

"I think I have a pretty good idea." He leaned forward, and I held my breath. This was it. Carson Hale was going to kiss me.

His lips were only a breath away from mine, and my eyes fluttered closed.

"Allie," he said my name so softly that I thought I might have imagined it.

"Yes," I answered him. It was the only response I could give. Yes to whatever he wanted. Yes to whatever he would take. My answer had been yes long before I even realized it.

"All right! Two cherry snow cones, both with extra syrup." The sound of Bob's voice snapped me out of my stupor, and I opened my eyes to see Carson quickly backing away from me.

He jumped down from the counter before I could get a good look at this face.

"After all that shit you just talked about me getting cherry?"

He grabbed the snow cones out of Bob's hands before turning back to me with a wink. He was completely unaffected by what had just happened between us. By what I had almost let happen. "Like you said, I've tried my fair share of flavors."

My stomach dropped, but I tried my hardest to control my features. The last thing I needed was him knowing how much he affected me. He already knew how affected I was by his cruelty, but I wouldn't let him have this. I refused to let him know how much I was bothered by him almost being more.

He handed me my snow cone, and I was careful not to let his fingers touch mine. I couldn't handle it right now. I couldn't handle his smirks or charm or the way he was looking at me.

"Thank you, Bob." I took a bite of my snow cone and

practically melted on the counter. "It's just as delicious as I remember."

"You're welcome." Bob grinned, and it was odd for such a burly man to feel so lovable. "But you don't stay away for so long again or next time I'm going to have to charge you for those."

"I won't." I chuckled and gave him a three-fingered Girl Scout salute. "Promise."

I climbed down from the counter as Carson walked past me and toward the door. "Thanks, dude. We'll eat these outside and get out of your way so you can get home."

He waved his hand as if it was no big deal. "You two be good."

"We will," I answered just as Carson said, "Not a chance in hell."

I knocked my shoulder into his and moved past him to the door. I pushed outside, the warm, humid air hitting me immediately. We weren't too close to the beach now, but you could still smell the saltwater in the air, could practically feel it on your skin.

"Where to now?" I ate a giant bite of my snow cone and dropped some on my chest. "Dang it." I used my finger to clean it up before it could reach my shirt and shoved my finger in my mouth.

When I looked up at Carson, he was watching my mouth like he was mesmerized.

"Hello? Are we done for the night? Was this the last stop?"

His gaze snapped up to mine, and I shoved another spoonful of snow cone in my mouth.

"No way, but you're not getting back in my car with that thing. You are too messy of an eater."

"I am not." I licked the edge of my cone where the syrup was starting to leak down the side.

"Yes. You are. You'll have my car ruined in no time."

I rolled my eyes because it was just a dang car. "All you Prep boys are all the same. Your daddy will just buy you a new car if it gets dirty."

What I said was meant as a joke, but there was a second of anger that passed over his face.

"You would know, huh?" He leaned against the hood of his car and crossed his ankles.

"Oh, yes," I said dramatically. "I know we don't know much about each other anymore, but I definitely make my rounds with the Prep boys. Haven't you heard?"

He paused; his bite of snow cone held halfway to his mouth. "First of all, I have heard."

I scoffed because he had lost his damn mind.

"I've heard the way they all talk about you. The way they are all interested in the elusive Allie Taylor."

"I am not elusive."

He finally took a bite of his snow cone and watched me. "Secondly, I still know plenty about you. I see you all the time now that Beck and Josie are dating."

"Seeing me and knowing me are two different things." He used to know me once upon a time. He knew me better than anyone.

"I know you."

"No. You don't." I looked him over. There was so much about him that had changed. There were things that were the same too, but even those things felt foreign now. "I don't know you either. Frankie knows you better than I do. Heck, even Josie does, and she's lived here for less than a year."

"What do you want to know?" He looked so cool and

calm as he asked me that, but I knew that he wasn't. There were things that he would refuse to talk about. The things he wanted to pretend didn't happen.

And they were the things I wanted to talk about most. I wanted to ask him about his parents, about his mom. I wanted to know what being at home was like for him now. Did he hate it more now than he did back then? Was it better?

But those questions didn't belong to me anymore. I didn't have the privilege of knowing those things about him, but part of me wondered if anyone did. Did he talk to Beck or Olly or Frankie about what had happened, or did he just smile and pretend like he was this perfect guy with his perfect little life.

"I don't know." I tucked my hand in my pocket and tried to think of something I wanted to know that wouldn't piss him off. "How long have you been dating your new girlfriend?"

He smirked, and it was so mesmerizing. It didn't matter that it was probably fake, and it was probably the same exact smile he gave to every other girl, it still made me want to fall into his chaos.

"She's not my girlfriend." He rubbed at the stubble on his chin. "I don't really do the whole girlfriend thing. You know that."

"Actually, I don't." I shrugged my shoulders. "I try to avoid any conversations about your love life if possible."

He cocked his head to the side and watched me. "Jealous?"

"Absolutely not." He could probably see straight through my lie. "It's just not something I really want to hear about."

He chuckled, and it grated on my nerves. "Would you

want to hear about me with some guy you knew? Or multiple guys, for that matter?"

He clenched his jaw, and I already had my answer before he even spoke. "No. I don't think that I would."

"Exactly. You were my childhood best friend. The last thing I want to hear about is your..." I waved toward his junk. The last conversation I overheard about him was exactly that. How good he was. How his moves on the baseball field weren't limited to that diamond. How he fucked like a champion, but he never kissed.

I didn't know whether I believed that last fact. I didn't want to. Was Carson so messed up that he didn't even kiss the girls he was with? Was he that damaged?

"My cock? You can say it, you know." He chuckled again, and I could feel my face heating. "I don't have any issue with you thinking about my cock if you want to."

"Thank you for being so selfless, but I think I'm good."

He stood and nodded toward his car. "Come on. Let's get out of here."

I tossed my empty snow cone into the trash can before following him. "Where are we heading now?"

"Wherever the hell we want." He opened his door and grinned at me over the hood. "You still have a night full of yeses to give me."

CHAPTER 9

CARSON

My phone went off in my pocket for the millionth time. Olly had been blowing me up to see what the hell I was doing, and after I snuck a picture of Allie eating her snow cone and sent it to him, Frankie started blowing me up.

I didn't read any of her messages, though. I already knew what kind of threats were probably waiting for me there regarding her friend, but she barely even knew Allie. Allie didn't need to be protected from me. She was a big girl, and even though she tried to act innocent, she knew exactly what she was doing.

I was certain of it.

She knew that she was driving me crazy with the whole Eli thing tonight. She knew how to get under my skin.

And she did. Every move she made, every time she said something stupid like I didn't know her.

I fucking knew her.

I knew her better than any of these people she puts on a show for. She wasn't as perfect as she made them believe.

"Do you need to get that?" Allie looked toward my pocket where my phone kept buzzing.

"No." I drove down the street without thinking. "I'm pretty sure it's just Frankie threatening to cut my balls off if I let something happen to you tonight."

"You told Frankie that we were together?"

"No." I tapped my fingers against the steering wheel. "I told Olly, and if you haven't noticed, those two don't keep any secrets from one another." Then the thought hit me. "Was I not supposed to tell them? Do you not want her to know that you're with me?"

"No. I don't care." She laughed, and I looked over just as she was messing with the edge of her shorts.

They were short enough to show off her perfect thighs, and I wanted to bury my fingers in them. I wanted to see what they would look like covered in the marks of my hands on her.

"I'm sure she'll have questions, though. This is a bit odd." She waved back and forth between us. "You're my enemy, and here I am out getting snow cones and surfing and doing whatever else you come up with after my date with someone else."

"I'm your enemy?" I cocked a brow.

"Well, you aren't exactly my friend." She narrowed her eyes at me. "If anyone heard the way you normally talk to me, they would call me a masochist for doing anything with you."

"It's not that bad, is it?" It was. I was cruel to her. We both knew it, but most days I couldn't help it. It was the only way I could stand to be around her.

"It is." She looked out the window, and I wished she

would just look at me. I wanted her to yell and scream and tell me how much of an ass I had been, but she never did. She just took it.

And that just pissed me off more.

Because I knew that she did so because she felt some sort of guilt over what happened between us. Some part of her, I didn't know how small, still cared about me in some way. And it was so fucked up.

I turned down the old back road we used to frequent all the time as kids, and Allie looked back to me.

"Where are we going?" There was a bit of panic in her voice, and I knew why. She hated this place with a passion.

"The old Sneed mansion."

The old house wasn't really a mansion, but it was close and it had always seemed like one when we were young. The legend was that the place was haunted. Some said the old man's wife had died inside. Others said that it had been haunted for decades.

All I knew was that this place had always scared the hell out of her, and I used to force her here with the rest of our friends because it meant she would hold my hand like it was her lifeline.

She would never say no because she didn't want anyone to know she was scared. She had always been a brave thing usually to a fault.

"I am not going in there." She settled into her seat and crossed her arms with an attitude.

"You have to say yes. It's a part of the deal."

"Not to this." She pointed out the window as I pulled onto the dark dirt road.

There were no streetlights, and the house was

completely blocked off by a large fence. I hadn't been here in years, not since the last time I came with her, and I didn't even know if the house was still standing.

The last time we were here, it was barely hanging on.

"How long has it been since we've been in there? We need to write our name on the wall."

The infamous wall that we all used to dare each other to sign our names on. We have done it at least a dozen times already, but it was normally during the day, and we normally had a crowd with us.

"I don't care, Carson. I'm not going in there."

"You seriously can't still be scared of this place." I slowed my car as we finally made our way toward the front gate, and I pulled off on the side of the road and cut my lights.

It was so dark that I could barely make out the tall fence to my side, and I knew that there was probably no way in hell I was going to actually talk her into this. But that was fine. Let her say no.

Without her yes, our deal was off, and she wouldn't be able to say a word when I continued to ruin her dates with that douchebag.

"Fine." She unbuckled her seat belt and leaned forward to look out the windshield. "Do you have a pen?"

"I do." I chuckled and leaned forward to pull a pen out of my glove compartment. My hand skimmed past her leg as I reached inside, and I tried to pretend like I didn't hear the way her breathing changed just slightly when we touched. Or how my dick hardened almost instantly.

I flipped the pen between my fingers for her to see before tugging it into my pocket.

"Are we really going to do this?"

"Yes." She was trying to psych herself up. "Let's go before I lose my nerve."

She climbed out of the car with a nervous smile on her face, and I realized that this might have been the best idea I had all night.

CHAPTER 10
ALLIE

Letting Carson talk me into anything was a bad idea.

I already knew that, but this was probably taking it to the extreme.

It was pitch-black, I was tiptoeing through the overgrown grass, and I couldn't stop giggling.

"You're going to get us caught." Carson looked back at me over his shoulder, but for a guy who was reprimanding me, he had a big smile on his face.

"We probably shouldn't be doing this at all." We finally made it to the old wooden fence, and I attempted to peek through the broken slats to get a good look at the house. It was so dark, I could barely see a thing, and the memories of how scared I used to get when we did this in the past crept up my spine. "Actually, this is a terrible idea. Let's go back."

"Do not be a chicken, Allie. We used to do this all the time." Carson bent down on one knee near the fence.

"I was a lot more gullible then, and I would let you talk me into anything." I stared at the house again, and parts of it looked like they were ready to fall at any given moment.

Carson patted his other knee for me to step on. "I don't want to go over there first."

"Can you jump this fence without me?" He cocked his head and watched me, and we both already knew the answer to that question.

"I could try." There was no way I would make it over that fence without his help.

"Go ahead then." He nodded to the fence. "Your head barely reaches the top of it, but be my guest."

I rolled my eyes and stepped my foot onto his thigh as I gripped the edge of the fence. "I'm not as light as I used to be."

Carson's hand came down on my ass, and I squealed and spun around to face him. I could not believe he just smacked my ass.

"Get your ass up there. I've got you."

I hated his words and the false security they gave me, but I didn't question him. I gripped the top of the fence in my hands and lifted myself up until both of my feet were balanced on Carson's thigh. Then I hoisted myself up and over the fence.

It wasn't graceful. My right knee hit the top of the fence with a thud, my shirt caught onto the fence, and I hit the ground on the other side without a single chance of bracing myself for the fall.

"I think I'm dead." I laid on my back and stared up at the stars as Carson jumped the fence.

He landed on his feet beside me, and I knew he was smiling without even looking at him.

"You ripped your shirt."

I nodded. "I think I ripped my dignity too."

"Come on." He chuckled and held his hand out to me.

I slid my hand in his and let him pull me up before dusting the grass and dirt from my clothes. He was right. My shirt was ripped across my stomach, but it could have been worse.

Carson used the flashlight on his phone to lead the way into the house, and I stayed practically attached to his back as I followed his steps.

"I don't remember it being this creepy when we were younger," I whispered and buried my fist in the back of his t-shirt.

"I've heard that some cults have been doing seances and shit in here."

"What?" I practically screeched and stopped dead in my tracks.

Carson chuckled like playing with the dead was a laughing matter. "Come on."

"Absolutely not. I'm not going in there now." I pointed to the house, and I swear it felt like someone or something was watching me.

"You should have decided that before we jumped the fence."

"You should have given me those details before we jumped the fence. It would have saved us a lot of time and my shirt."

Carson grabbed my hand in his and tugged me forward.

I dug my heels into the ground and tried to pull away. "I'm not kidding. I'm not going."

"Yes. You are." He stepped closer to me, blocking my view of the house. "You already said yes."

"And I can change my mind." I waved my hand up toward the house. "You're right. I'm boring. I admit it. You can give me shit about it and wreck my plans with Eli. I don't care. I'm not going in there."

Carson bent and his shoulder hit my stomach before I could realize what was going on. His arm wrapped around the back of my thighs, and he lifted me over his shoulder.

"Carson, no!" I smacked his back just as he took off walking toward the house. "I will never forgive you for this."

"That's all right. We're not even friends, remember?" He used my words against me. "You can be mad at me all you want to."

He started up the old wooden stairs, and I clung to his back for support. I would never forgive him for forcing me into this old haunted house, but I really wouldn't forgive him if he dropped me.

We reached the top of the stairs and the porch creaked under our weight. His hands moved to my hips, and he slowly slid me down his body and onto the floor. We were about to be murdered by ghosts or rabid animals or something, but suddenly I couldn't bring myself to care.

I couldn't think about anything other than the hard planes of his body beneath mine, or the way his hands still rested on my hips. I looked up at him as he stared down at me, and my stomach was so tight that I felt like I was on the verge of snapping.

I still hated Carson Hale, but I also wanted him.

Even now, after he had forced me onto this dang porch and hadn't listened to a word I said. I still wanted him.

"See, you made it up here and nothing has happened yet."

"Yet." I annunciated the word. "But when something in here kills me, make sure to tell my parents that I loved them."

He chuckled and his hands tightened on my hips. It was almost unnoticeable, as if he hadn't meant to do it, but I noticed. "What about Eli? Anything I should tell him?"

"Tell him that he was the last thing I thought of when I died." I sighed dramatically, and I knew it would get under Carson's skin.

"You're so full of shit."

"Maybe." I shrugged and stepped back out of his reach. "Maybe not. But I don't need everyone to think I died some lonely hermit who didn't even get any dates before she croaked."

Carson passed by me and toward the door. "You are seriously insane. You could go on plenty of dates, but you are never interested."

"Not true."

The door creaked open, and I peeked around Carson's shoulder. I couldn't see anything inside except where his flashlight shone, but it looked almost exactly like I remembered it.

"It is. You just don't care to notice all the guys who are interested in you."

"Okay." I followed him over the threshold and stood directly behind him as he shined the light around the old living room. There was a dusty blanket on the floor and cobwebs were still the main source of decoration. "The only guys who are interested in me are self-centered jocks and guys who only want to get laid."

"Ouch." Carson rubbed his chest and looked back at me. "You know I'm a jock, right."

"Prime example."

"Whatever." He rolled his eyes and moved further into the house. "Eli's a jock too."

"Yeah, but he's not a starter, so he's not as egotistical as the rest of you."

"Oh shit." He bent over and laughed so hard that I thought something might be wrong with him. "I cannot believe you just dissed your boyfriend like that."

"That's not a diss. That's the truth, and he's not my boyfriend."

"I'm sure if the poor guy heard that the only reason you agreed to go out with him is because he rides the bench, he wouldn't take it very well."

"I didn't say that."

"Basically." He spun around to face me just as we reached the old stairwell that looked like a deathtrap. "Is that why you said no to me when I asked? Because I'm a star player?"

"See." I pointed my finger at him as I checked behind me to make sure I wasn't about to be attacked. "That's the exact attitude I'm talking about. Such a turn-off."

He rolled his eyes, but I continued. "But no, I could name about a hundred different reasons I said no to you."

"Give me one." He suddenly sounded so serious.

"What?" I swear I saw something move behind me. "I don't think this is the place. Let's write our dang names on the wall and get out of here."

"No." He crossed his arms and stood his ground. "We're not going anywhere until you tell me."

"Oh. I don't know." I held up my hand and started listing reasons on my fingers. "You're a jerk. You treat me like you hate me. You used to be my best friend. You haven't really talked to me since that day when I should have been there for you." I was getting pissed with every reason I listed. "You never gave me a chance. I've always been the last girl you would ever be interested in."

He moved toward me, and I backed away with every step he made.

"You're such an idiot."

My back hit the wall just as his words hit me.

"Oh, and you tell me I'm an idiot like that would somehow make me want to date you."

His chest hit mine, and he looked as angry as I felt. "Well, you're acting like one."

I pushed against his chest, trying to force him away from me, but he didn't budge. "You're acting like one. You think after all this time of you treating me like I never mattered to you, I would suddenly just forget that any of it ever happened."

"You say that you were the last girl I would be interested in like that would somehow make it true. Like I didn't used to follow you around like a lovesick puppy."

I could barely catch my breath as he spoke. I had no idea what he was saying. He had no idea. He couldn't say things like that to mess with my head when we both knew they weren't true.

I stared at him, and he stared at me. Neither one of us wanted to face the truth of us. Neither was ready for the chaos that conversation would bring.

"I know you have some sick obsession with me never dating Eli, or anyone for that matter, but you don't have to say stuff like that to me." I looked away from him, but he brought his hand to my face and used his fingers on my jaw to force me to face him again.

"You're right. I don't want you to date him."

I opened my mouth to tell him that fact was perfectly clear, but he pressed his thumbs to my lips to stop me.

"But I'm not saying anything that isn't true." He stared into my eyes before his gaze fell to my lips. Everything about him felt dangerous at that moment. The look in his eyes, the sharpness of his breaths, the way his thumb pressed into my lips almost painfully.

He looked predatory and ravenous, and I knew that I would let him have whatever he wanted. If Carson was willing to take from me, then I was more than willing to give.

My chest brushed against his repeatedly as my breaths rushed in and out of my lungs.

"You were my best friend," I whispered against his thumb. I had no idea why I said it, but I felt like neither of us had acknowledged that fact in so long. I felt like we had forgotten who we were.

"I was." He nodded and leaned forward. The heat of him surrounded me as he ran his nose along my jaw.

I held my breath and tried not to move. I focused only on the parts of my body that he was touching, and I wanted to scream. I wanted to beg him to stop. I wanted to demand more.

"But I haven't been your best friend for a long time. Have I?"

I shook my head because I could get an answer out if I tried.

His hand on my mouth moved back to my jaw, and he used it to tilt my head to the side and give him more room. His face moved over the length of my neck, barely-there touches that made me squirm beneath his touch until his lips gently pressed over my rapidly beating pulse.

"So, we can't use that as an excuse anymore." His tongue

traced over the spot where his lips had just been, and my hips surged forward against his.

Everything inside me felt like it was being pulled so tightly. One small move and I would snap. One touch from him and I was liable to fall apart.

"You're not the same Allie that I was too damn scared to tell her I liked her, and I'm not the same Carson that always wanted to be there for you." He peppered more kisses against my neck, and his other hand wrapped around my back. He flattened his palm against the small of my back and force my body impossibly closer to his.

"You have no idea what I wanted from you."

"Oh, yeah?" He leaned back slightly and looked up at me through his dark lashes. "Did you want this?"

He kissed the very base of my throat and I swallowed hard and deep against his lips.

"What about this?" His lips trailed lower and lower, his skin pressing into mine as he went, his tongue leaving a trail of chill bumps.

His hand tightened against my jaw as his teeth grazed the top of my breast, and I couldn't stop the small whimper that seemed to echo around us.

"Did you ever think about what it would be like for me to taste your skin?" He pressed his hips into mine, and I could feel how hard he was. "For me to taste your pussy?"

"Carson." His name was a plea on my lips, and I sounded so desperate for him.

"What, Allie?" He moved his hand from my jaw and slowly ran it down my chest. He cupped my breast over my shirt as he stared down at his hand, then he tugged the edge of my shirt down with a rough jerk. "Do you want me to stop?"

I shook my head again and stared down at him. My thin black bra was fully visible for him, and I wanted him to move it too. I wanted every single thing that stood between us to disappear.

"Tell me, Allie. I need to hear you say it."

"Please don't stop," I answered him immediately.

He looked up at me for only a moment before his tongue slipped under my bra and slid across my nipple. He stared at me the whole time, taking in my reaction, watching my face as I wanted to beg him for more.

I didn't need to give him any more words, though. He kneaded one of my breasts in his hand as he tasted the other. Each sensation feeling better than the other, my body at war as he pinched my nipple between his fingers then soothed my other one with his tongue.

Intense pressure built in my stomach, and I had only felt this way when I was alone. When I had taken my pleasure into my own hands and prayed that my parents couldn't hear me.

I had never been touched like this by anyone else.

"Oh, God. Please, Carson."

He dropped onto his knees almost instantly. He pressed kisses to my stomach, his lips finding my skin that was exposed from the rip in my shirt, as his fingers moved to the button of my shorts. I didn't know if I was ready for this. Especially with Carson, a boy who only seemed to forget he hated me for this one night, but there was no way that I was stopping him.

He tugged my shorts and panties down my thighs in one movement, and I looked up at the ceiling to hide my embarrassment. Carson had been with plenty of girls. I was well aware of that fact.

And it made me feel so self-conscious.

"Look at me, Allie."

I jerked my gaze back to him. He was on his knees before me, his hands pressing into my thighs, his eyes only on me, and I had never experienced something so potent in all my life.

He didn't move his gaze away from mine as he pressed a tender kiss to the top of my thigh, and he still didn't look away as he moved his mouth to the top of my pussy and kissed me there like it was the most natural thing.

His eyes darkened, and he pressed his tongue into the seam of me, tasting the wetness that I knew was waiting there for him. I had never been so wet before.

"Fuck, Allie." He finally looked away as he tasted me again. There was no more gentleness or teasing. His hands moved to my ass, forcing me forward against his mouth as my shoulders pressed into the wall, and he dove into my flesh like he was starving for me. "You are so fucking wet."

"I'm sorry," I stammered and clenched my hands at my sides.

"Sorry?" Carson chuckled against my pussy, and my knees threatened to buckle. "It's the sexiest fucking thing I've ever seen. You are the best goddamned thing I have ever tasted."

His hands pressed into my hips and forced me to turn around. I wasn't ready, almost tripping over my own feet, my legs still trapped with my shorts and panties around my thighs, but Carson didn't care. He pulled my hips backward, my arms catching the wall to hold me up, and for a moment, I finally remembered where we were.

"We shouldn't be doing this here." I pushed my ass out even as I spoke. "This isn't right."

"Stop thinking, Allie." He ran his tongue from the front of my pussy to the seam of my ass, and I almost died.

"Oh my God." I dug my elbows into the wall, praying that they and this old damn house would be strong enough to hold me up long enough to take whatever Carson was going to give me.

"That's it." He ate my pussy. His tongue a whirlwind against my wet skin, his lips sucking my clit into his mouth, and I knew that I wasn't going to make it. I moved my hips against his face, too far gone to be embarrassed.

"Yes, baby. Ride my face. Show me exactly how you'd take my cock."

I slammed my eyes shut as I let his words wash over me. He was so dirty and forward, and it was so damn arousing.

He spread my ass cheeks apart as I arched my back harder, giving him better access to anything he wanted, and he slid his tongue inside me over and over. I whimpered, and he moaned. The sound reverberating through my body.

His fingers dug into my ass, the feeling of them on the edge of pain, as he flicked his tongue against my clit.

"One day, I'm going to fuck this perfect ass of yours too." His hands inched closer to the parts of my body no one had ever been, and I tensed. "Has anyone ever been in there, baby, or will I be the first one?"

"No." I tried to shake my head against the wall, but I could barely concentrate on what he was saying. "No one has ever."

I cried out as his mouth pulled my clit inside it, and I almost fell to the ground as he sucked the sensitive bud over and over again. He knew the exact pressure to use, the exact speed, and I forced myself to let go as the orgasm he was wringing from my body racked through every part of me.

I didn't know if I was crying out or screaming or begging him in words that didn't make any sense, but Carson braced my hips in his hands as he slowly brought me down from my high. His lips pressed against the back of my thighs; the skin so sensitive it caused me to jolt forward.

I could feel him standing behind me, his hands never leaving my body, and as my heart rate started to come back down, the reality of what we had just done started to creep its way in.

But Carson wasn't freaking out.

He wrapped his arms around me and slowly brought his hand down to cup over my pussy. I was still so wet from me and his mouth, and his fingers moved over the moisture and my sensitive skin.

"Tell me this is mine, Allie. I need to hear you say it before I bend you over and fuck you."

My stomach tightened again and I opened my mouth to tell him the truth. I was ready to tell him that I had always been his.

But a loud thump startled us both, and I screamed as a flashlight shone directly in our faces.

"This is the Clermont Bay Police Department. You are trespassing on private property."

"Oh my God." I scrambled to tug my panties and shorts up my legs as my heart felt like it was going to beat out of my chest.

"Fuck." Carson moved his body to block the view of mine, and he helped me as I fumbled with my shaking hands.

"I need the both of you to step over to this side of the house." The officer's voice was firm and irritated, and I felt like I was going to die.

"Give us just a damn minute." Carson didn't care. He spun me toward him and quickly buttoned my shorts before anyone else could see anything. Once they were situated, he tugged my shirt back into place then stared up at me.

The look he gave me felt like he was trying to say so much, but I didn't understand a word of it. I was too overwhelmed with this place, with him, with what he had just done, and now with the second police officer that had just entered the house.

"I'm not going to tell you all again. Move to this side of the house."

Carson gripped my hand in his and held it tightly as we made our way over in front of the two officers.

"Is there anyone else here or just you two?"

"Just us," Carson answered, and he sounded so annoyed. There wasn't an ounce of fear in his voice.

I clung to his hand because I was scared. I'd just had the most earth-shattering moment of my life, and I still hadn't calmed down from it. I still hadn't comprehended the fact that I was holding Carson's hand in the middle of a haunted house, with two police officers staring at us, and all I could think about was the way I could still practically feel his tongue against my skin.

"What are the two of you doing in here?" One of the officers shined his flashlight back and forth between us, and I could barely make out his face through the blinding light.

"We were just..." I hesitated because I had no idea what to say, but Carson quickly answered for me.

"We were just seeing if this place was really haunted."

One of the officers cursed under his breath. "Well, I hate to tell you this, but Mr. Sneed doesn't take kindly to people trespassing on his property. He wants us to arrest you."

"You've got to be fucking kidding me."

"Watch your mouth, son." The older officer, who I could now see, barked at Carson and shined his light directly in his face. "Let's get these two separated and call their parents."

"You're not taking her anywhere." Carson's hand tightened around mine, and I moved closer to him. "She's with me."

"I don't think you understand how this works. You're trespassing on private property in the middle of the night, and I don't want to have to tell your parents what I'm pretty sure I walked in on."

I buried my face into Carson's arm because I was about to die of embarrassment. "It's fine, Carson. I'll go with them."

I stepped away from him, trying to release his hand, but he refused.

"No." His hand held firmly in mine. "They can call our parents while we're together."

"Don't make me arrest you both tonight. I don't want to do the paperwork."

I tugged my hand out of Carson's again, but he didn't budge. "Let me go, Carson. I can't get in trouble." I couldn't afford any sort of blemish on my record. Every college scholarship I had been working so hard to get would be in jeopardy.

"No." He shook his head and stared down at me. He opened his mouth to say something, something I desperately wanted to hear, but the officers were already on us. One pulled Carson's arm behind his back before he forced his hand away from mine, and I watched in horror as he put Carson's wrists in handcuffs.

"Is this really necessary?" I practically yelled just as an old man walked through the front door of the house. He looked back and forth between me and Carson, and he looked so angry.

I shut my mouth just as his gaze landed back on me.

"I want them both arrested and charges pressed." He grumbled and my stomach dropped.

"They're just a couple of kids." The officer who now held my arm tried to reason with him. "Let us just get them home. They won't do this again."

"No." He shook his head, and I searched the room for Carson's face.

"I want to call my dad." He tried to tug his arms forward, but the officer gave him no leeway.

"Oh, you pussy," the old man muttered, and if I wasn't shaking, I would have laughed. "You're brave enough to break into this home in the middle of the night, but you need your daddy to help you get out of it."

I could see the anger brewing in Carson's face, and I knew that he was about to lose it.

"We didn't think anyone lived here. We honestly didn't mean to cause any trouble."

"Well, you did." He looked back and forth between me and Carson. "I'm sick and tired of you rich little assholes thinking you can come onto someone else's property and ruin things and do whatever you want without any consequences."

"Please." My voice was in a near panic. "Let them call my parents. We'll do community service or whatever you need, but please, I cannot get arrested."

"Stop talking, Allie. My dad will get us out of this." Carson was stone-faced, and I knew that he was probably right. His dad could most definitely get him out of this, but he didn't owe me anything and I couldn't take the chance.

So, I ignored him and kept talking. "I have a scholarship riding on the fact that the rest of my senior year goes perfectly. I cannot afford to lose it. I will do whatever you need."

The old man stared at me for a few minutes before looking up to the officer at my side.

"It's up to you, Mr. Sneed." He shrugged his shoulders. "But we have a busy night ahead of us, so I need you to make a decision now."

Mr. Sneed raised his hand and pointed a finger at me before pointing it back at Carson. "You will both be here tomorrow after school. If you're so fascinated with this place, then you can help me clean it up."

"Hell no." Carson shook his head, but I ignored him and winced.

"Can it be the next day? I have work tomorrow."

"Fine." He looked away from me and spoke to the officers. "Have their parents pick them up, and I want their word that they'll be here. Both of them."

"And how long will we have to do this crap?" Carson grumbled. "I have baseball."

"Until I decide you're done." Mr. Sneed wasn't taking any of Carson's shit. "I won't interfere with school or your jobs, but after all that, you're to be here."

"Deal," I answered before Carson could screw this up for me.

"The both of you," he reiterated. "You both show up or I'll go forward on pressing charges."

"We'll be here."

CHAPTER 11
CARSON

By the time our parents got out to the old Sneed property, I was ready to kill the old man, and Allie for not shutting her mouth. My dad could have gotten us out of all of this, but she somehow agreed to make us do labor for the old man to keep us out of trouble.

She was insane.

"I'm not doing it," I said to my dad just as he and Allie's parents made their way back over to us.

"Unfortunately, son. Yes, you are." My dad was pressing buttons on his phone and not even looking up at me. "It appears Allie has already agreed to the arrangement for both of you, and Mr. Sneed isn't interested in any sort of payment to get you out of it."

"I'm sorry." Allie looked up at her dad who had his arm around her shoulders. "I freaked out because I don't want to lose my scholarship."

"It's okay." Allie's mom's smile was weak. "What were you two doing out here anyway?"

"Yes, Carson? What the hell were you thinking?"

"I don't see what the big deal is. We used to do this all the time." I pointed to the old house that I knew has at least a dozen of mine and Allie's signatures on the wall. "We just didn't get caught then."

"Well, you're not a kid anymore." My dad shoved his phone in his pocket and crossed his arms. "Making stupid fucking decisions isn't going to get you anywhere anymore. You're eighteen years old. It's time for you to grow up."

Every single word he said felt like acid in my veins. The man barely spoke to me anymore, we rarely even saw each other, and he wanted to give me a lecture on who I should be? I would have hated every second of it even if he wasn't doing it in front of Allie and her parents, but that only made it worse. It made me want to slam my fist into his face and demand he shut up.

He had no idea how a man should act.

"I wanted to see if it was really haunted," Allie lied so easily, and she avoided looking at me. "I talked Carson into coming here."

"That's a lie." I shook my head.

"No. It's not." She looked from her parents to my dad. "Carson told me it was a bad idea, but I wanted to see if it was still as scary as it used to be. I take full responsibility."

I stared at her, but she refused to look at me. I didn't know what she was doing, but I didn't need her to save me. If that's what she thought she was doing, she was wrong.

"Unfortunately, you don't have that choice." My father turned his stern gaze to her. "Mr. Sneed is adamant that both of you come back here to work off whatever he deems necessary, and he isn't going to budge."

"Okay. Let's get home. It's already been a long night." Allie's dad ran his hand over the back of her head.

"Can I talk to Allie first?" I looked between them. "Can we just have a minute alone?"

"Of course." Allie's mom was watching my dad as she spoke. "Just make it quick, please."

I walked away from where they stood, over to where my car was still parked in the tall grass. I could hear Allie walking behind me, and everything seemed to come down on me all at once.

I hadn't planned our night to go like this. Not the police or the community service, and definitely not the part where I went down on her. But I couldn't stop any of it.

And now when I should have been worried about us getting into trouble, all I could think about was the way I could still taste her on my tongue and the way she had looked at me like she had never been touched like that in all her life.

It was intoxicating and infuriating, and it didn't accomplish anything that I needed to tonight. I just needed her to warm up to me, to warm up to the idea of possibly dating me. That was all I needed to keep Eli away from her. I needed her to choose me instead of him, but I got too distracted by the way she rode my tongue to remember any of that.

This wasn't real.

Allie and I would never be anything more than the past, and I needed to fucking remember that.

"What are you doing?" I whirled around to face her and leaned against my car.

"What do you mean?" She tucked a few of her blonde curls behind her ear. They were still wild from the ocean, the curls coming to life in a way they didn't when she tried to tame them, and the urge to bury my hand in them was overwhelming.

"That." I waved toward our parents. "I don't need you lying for me. I'm a big boy, Allie. I can handle myself."

She took a step back, and I tried to avoid the look of hurt on her face.

"I was just trying to help. Your dad was so pissed."

"I don't need your help." I chuckled and looked her up and down. "I'm not some guy who needs you to save me, Allie."

"I'm not trying to save you." She sounded so disgusted with me, and honestly, I didn't blame her. "I just didn't want..." She looked back over her shoulder at our parents.

"What, Allie? What don't you want?" I cocked my head to the side and stared at her. My head was pounding, and my chest ached, and I just wanted to get the hell out of here. I wanted to get as far away from everything as I could. I needed a joint and the ocean and to just get lost for a while. "My family isn't like yours, remember? We don't all have a perfect happily ever after."

"My family isn't perfect."

"No? Is your dad fucking anyone other than your mom?"

"Carson." My name was filled with so much sympathy, and I hated it.

I wished I hadn't even said that out loud. I knew that she knew, of course she did, but it wasn't something that we had ever talked about. I'd never had to watch her look at me with so much pity in her eyes.

"Don't worry about it." I chuckled without an ounce of humor. "I guess I will see you here in a couple days."

"Are we not going to even talk about what happened?"

She was so vulnerable, and I knew that I shouldn't have been a dick to her.

Not after everything that had just happened and what I was trying to accomplish, but I couldn't stand it. I felt trapped, and the only way to push myself out was to push everyone away.

"Which part?" I ran my gaze down her body, and God, she was so damn beautiful.

"Oh. I don't know," she huffed, and her hands balled into fists at her sides. "Maybe the part where you..." She trailed off, and I knew that she was too embarrassed to say it.

She had just let me do whatever I wanted with her body, and she couldn't even say the words.

"Made you come against my tongue."

"Yes," she whisper-shouted before turning to look over her shoulder, but our parents weren't close enough to hear us. "Do you think we should talk about that?"

"What is there to talk about?" I leaned forward and hooked my finger into the belt loop of her shorts. I tugged her toward me, and she shuffled on her feet until she was exactly where I wanted her. Her knees pressed against the inside of mine, and she looked so lost as she stared up at me.

"Maybe the fact that this isn't normal. You hate me. You..."

"I can hate you and still eat your pussy, Allie."

She huffed and tried to take a step back, but I refused to let her. Instead, I moved in closer, bringing my mouth to her ear as I spoke. "Did you not like it? You could have fucking fooled me."

"I didn't say that."

"Then what is it?" My lips touched her skin as I spoke,

and she shivered. "Has someone done it better than me? Is there someone else you'd rather be eating you?"

She shook her head, but I kept going. I was becoming intoxicated by the feel of her and the knowledge that she wanted me as much as I wanted her.

"When you let someone else go down on you, when they were fucking you, did you ever think of me?"

"No." Her answer hit me in the chest, but I didn't believe her.

"Well, I've thought about you. I've imagined exactly what you would look like underneath me, what you would taste like, the way you would sound when you screamed my name."

She turned her face closer to mine, and our mouths were so damn close. I had already fucked her pussy with my mouth, but I still hadn't tasted her lips. I hadn't kissed the girl I had been thinking about kissing since I was twelve years old.

"That's not what I meant."

"What isn't?" I pushed her hair over her shoulder and rested my hand on the base of her neck. I could feel the rapid beat of her pulse and the way she swallowed nervously like she was scared to tell me whatever she was going to say next.

"I've thought about you," she said it so quietly I almost missed it. "But I've never." She looked away, but I moved my hand to her chin and forced her to look back at me. "I've never had anyone else touch me like that."

"You've never had anyone else eat you out?" Fuck, the thought of me being the first one to ever taste her did something to me. It made me feel so damn possessive. I never wanted anyone else to touch her ever again.

Even if I knew how unrealistic that was.

"No." She shook her head. "No one else has ever touched me at all."

I jerked back from her and stared into her eyes as my heart felt like it was going to beat out of my chest. "You're a virgin?"

"My parents are right there, Carson."

As soon as she said the words, her mom started making her way toward us. "Allie, it's time to head home."

"Okay," Allie answered her mom before staring back at me. "I will see you later."

"Why didn't you tell me?" I couldn't focus on anything other than the fact that she was a virgin, that no one but me had ever touched her.

"It's not really something I like to broadcast." She crossed her arms over her chest. "Plus, it's not like I had the opportunity."

"I would have..."

"What? What would you have done, Carson?"

"I don't know." Fuck, I would have probably started by actually kissing her. "I would have been gentler. I wouldn't have talked to you the way I did in there. I wouldn't have done all that." I waved my hand to the dilapidated house where I had just given her her first sexual experience.

God, I had asked her if she had ever let anyone fuck her in the ass. She had said no, but I hadn't realized that she meant at all. I hadn't realized how inexperienced she was.

"It's fine, Carson." She looked away from me and shook her head gently. "I don't need you to explain anything to me. It's perfectly clear that you regret what happened."

I did regret it, but not for the reason she thought. I regretted that this was the way I had treated her, even though knowing what I knew now, I wanted to do it again. I fucking ached to taste and touch and fuck every inch of her flawless body.

"I don't regret it."

She wasn't listening to me, though. She was already heading back to her parents, and I knew that she was going to hate me even more after tonight. She was going to hate me and regret letting me take anything from her.

"Allie," I called to her, frantic for her to hear me before she left.

She stopped for only a second, but she didn't turn back to me. "It's okay. I don't have any delusions about what we are." She tilted her head up, staring at the dark night sky before she spoke softly one last time. "Don't treat me differently than the rest of them. I'm no different. We can go right back to pretending like we don't know anything about one another."

CHAPTER 12
ALLIE

"You have to be there by four-thirty?" Josie huffed over the phone. "That is so unfair. How long are you all going to have to do this?"

"I'm honestly not sure." I turned down the old back road and slowed my car. It was already almost four-twenty, and I refused to be late. "I guess until Mr. Sneed is content that we've made up for trespassing on his property."

"I still can't believe you volunteered you both for that. Carson's not happy."

"Well, it was really the only option I had, and Carson can kiss my ass." The thoughts of what he had done to me the last time we were here flashed through my mind, but I tried to shake them off. I didn't have time to think about that.

It was a mistake, and it never should have happened.

I would never let it happen again.

I saw the way he looked at me when I told him I was a virgin. He was shocked and something else. Freaked out, maybe. Whatever it was, that look on his face was perfectly clear about one thing. He regretted it.

And I shouldn't have been surprised.

Everything I had ever heard about Carson from other girls was that he was nothing more than a good time. He never kissed on the mouth, and he was even less likely to come back for more.

Carson didn't have girlfriends or fuck buddies or anything in between. He just fucked whoever he wanted to, then he moved on.

That thought made my chest feel like it was caving in, and not for me. I could handle Carson never wanting to do anything with me or touch me in any way again.

I would crave it like crazy. Every time I saw him, I knew it would be the thing that constantly haunted my mind, but it didn't matter.

What bothered me the most was that Carson could pretend like this was who he was. He could make himself believe that this was all he was worth.

"Yeah. I'm sure he'd love to." Josie laughed and guilt washed over me as I pulled into the old gravel driveway and stopped at the gate.

I hadn't told Josie or Frankie about what happened the other night. Of course, they knew about the cops and the agreement I made with Mr. Sneed to keep us out of trouble, but I didn't tell either of them about what happened before that.

I couldn't tell them about how I let Carson put his mouth on my body even though he didn't even attempt to kiss my lips. I didn't want to face the fact that even though I didn't want to admit it, I always held on to the belief that I was still more important to Carson than any of these other girls.

He treated me like he hated me, but I still held on to hope that deep down, he still loved me as the best friends that we were. It was stupid and immature, and I didn't want to see that truth staring back at me in my friends' faces.

"I just pulled in." I put my car in park and looked around. I didn't see Carson's car or any sign of Mr. Sneed. "I'll call you when it's over if Carson and I don't kill each other."

"Okay. But do not let him be an ass to you. I will kill him myself if I have to."

I chuckled and leaned my head back against my headrest. She would do it. I knew she would.

"I won't. Promise." I just had to repeat that over and over to myself. I wouldn't let him be anything to me. Not a jerk or a flirt or a guy who I couldn't stop thinking about.

Carson Hale was nothing to me anymore, and I needed to make sure it stayed that way.

"All right. Call me when you're done."

"I will."

"Bye."

I hung up my phone and let it fall to my lap. "You can do this, Allie."

A knock on my window had me jumping out of my skin, and when I looked up, Carson was leaning down to look in my car. He opened my door before I could and stared down at me.

"Were you just talking to yourself?"

That's the first thing he's going to say to me after what happened the other night? I hadn't talked to him since I walked away from him that night, and I hadn't wanted to. Avoiding him was the best option.

"I was on the phone."

"Yeah. I saw that, but I meant after your phone call."

"When did you get here?" I looked around and finally

noticed his car parked on the edge of the driveway behind mine. "I didn't see you pull in."

"You should really watch your surroundings better." He leaned farther into my car and whispered, "We are at a haunted house, you know."

"Stop." I pulled my keys out of the ignition and climbed out of my car. He didn't back up or give me space as I tried to pass him, and if I wasn't mistaken, there was the slightest hint of a smirk on his face as he watched me try to avoid touching him. "This place is not haunted."

"They say it is." We both turned at the sound of Mr. Sneed's voice. He was walking up the driveway with a set of keys in his hand and a grimace on his face. "It's too bad none of the ghosts got to you all the other night, then I wouldn't have to be dealing with you both right now."

"We're really sorry." I pushed past Carson and made my way toward him. "We really didn't mean to cause you any trouble."

He picked up the heavy lock on the front gate in his hand, then looked over at me. "Would you all prefer to climb the fence like you did the other night?"

"No." I didn't bother to look at Carson as he answered. "Allie actually beefed it trying to get over the fence the other night, so you probably wouldn't get much work out of her if we did."

I swung my hand out to the side and connected with his stomach.

His loud grunt put a smile on my face.

Mr. Sneed rolled his eyes and unlocked the gate before pushing the creaking gate open. We followed him inside, stepping over sticks and overgrown grass.

"What exactly are you wanting us to do?" Carson looked

around and I knew he was probably thinking the same thing I was. This place was an absolute mess.

"For today." Mr. Sneed rubbed at his chin and followed Carson's gaze. "I want you all to work on getting this lawn cleaned up." He pointed toward the back of the house, and there was something about him that made me think he was so sad. "There's a shed in the back that has all sorts of tools that the two of you might need. I'll come back and check on the two of you in a few hours."

He didn't say another word before he pushed back through the gate then closed it shut behind him. Even in the broad daylight, the house still gave me the creeps, and the sound of the gate shutting made my skin crawl.

I just wanted to get this done and get out of here.

I didn't wait for Carson as I made my way to the back of the house. I found the shed easily enough, but the thing was even more decrepit than the house was. It took me a few tries to get the door pulled open and dust flew into my face.

"Hold on. Let me do that before you hurt yourself." Carson pulled the door from my hand, but I wasn't listening to him.

I pushed inside and was immediately met with a bunch of tools that looked like they were older than I was. I lifted the rusty wheelbarrow and pushed it back toward the door. The wheel was barely hanging on and that made it hard to push.

"Did you not hear anything I just said?" Carson growled and grabbed a few tools before following me out.

"I did. I just don't care." I shrugged my shoulders and kept walking.

"So, that's how we're going to act, huh?"

I stopped and turned to look at him. The sun was

directly in my eyes, and I lifted my hand to block it. "How exactly would you like me to act? Isn't this what we do?" I waved my other hand between the two of us.

"Is this what you want us to do?" He cocked his head and studied me, and that pissed me off more than his question.

"I really don't think it matters what I want."

"Of course, it does." He answered so quickly like he actually meant it, but I knew better than that. He didn't care about me or what I felt. If he did, we would still be friends. We wouldn't be this lost, messed-up pair of people who didn't even know how to act around each other anymore.

"Let's just get this done, Carson." I turned back to the wheelbarrow and pushed it to the front yard while he followed me. "I have about a million other things I'd rather be doing than this."

"Me too," he grumbled and set down his tools. He started picking up small sticks and broken pieces of limbs out of the yard before throwing them in the wheelbarrow. "I'm not sure if you remember this or not, but you're the one who got us roped into this."

"I'm pretty sure I wouldn't have gotten us roped into anything if you hadn't made me come out here in the first place." There was so much trash and debris that was almost hidden in the overgrown grass, and I wondered how much of it was from idiots like us who trespassed on the property.

"I didn't make you do anything. You were more than a willing participant."

I spun around to face him, but he was still working. He didn't even spare me a glance as he said, "You can pretend all you want that you didn't want to be here with me, but we both know you better than that. If you didn't want to, you would have said no." Finally, he looked up at me, and there was already a fine sheen of sweat on his brow. "If you didn't want me to touch you, you should have said so."

"I never said I didn't want you to." I shook my head because I didn't know what I was saying.

"Well, the way you're acting right now makes me think that you regret it." He rubbed his hand over his hair in frustration. "I had no clue you were a virgin, Allie, or I wouldn't have."

"Can we not talk about this?" I went back to my job and started picking up as much trash and sticks as I could carry.

"I think we need to talk about it. I never meant for this to get so out of hand."

"I get it, Carson." I dumped everything into the wheelbarrow with a loud thump. "I'm not really your usual type, but don't insult me. I have no interest in being anything more with you than what we are."

"Which is what?"

"I don't know." I huffed. "You tell me."

He stepped toward me, and I tensed. My stomach tightened just looking at him, and the last thing I needed was for him to be closer to me. But he didn't seem to notice.

"I think that what we are doesn't really matter. What matters" —he stared into my eyes before his gaze fell to my lips— "is that you clearly want me just as badly as I want you."

"Carson." I stepped back and almost tripped. Carson caught my arm in his hand, balancing me and holding me closer to him.

"You know that it's true. Tell me I'm wrong."

"It doesn't matter if it's true or not." I jerked my elbow from his grip. "Me and you don't work on any level. We didn't work as friends, and we sure as heck don't work as this." I motioned back and forth between us. "I think it would be best if we just do what we're supposed to be here to do, then go our separate ways. There doesn't need to be anything more."

"You really think we can do that?"

"We've done it before, haven't we? You've been pretending like I didn't exist for years now."

"That's true." He pushed against me so quickly that I didn't have time to react. That was what I was telling myself. I didn't willingly fall into his arms and let him hold me like I was capable of not letting it affect me. "But that was before I knew what you tasted like." He leaned forward, running his nose along my jaw. "I didn't know what you sounded like when you moaned my name."

"Carson, stop." I didn't sound like I wanted him to stop. My voice was breathy and desperate, and I sounded like I was begging him for more.

"Do you really want me to?" His hand tightened on my hip and my body pushed forward the tiniest bit as I leaned onto my toes. "Tell me you don't want this, and I'll stop. I won't bring it up again."

I took a deep breath and the smell of him overwhelmed me. He smelled so good. So intoxicating. There was a hint of his smoky cologne, but it mixed with a freshness that was wholly him. It was as if no matter how much he tried to wash it away, the smell of the ocean never left him.

It had become as much a part of him as he had become a part of it. It had been that way for as long as I had known him.

"You still smell like the ocean." I turned my head, and our faces became so close. Part of me wanted to lean forward and kiss him. I wanted to know if what everyone said about him was true. I was desperate to find out if he would push me away as it was rumored he had done with so many before me.

He chuckled and tangled his fingers in my hair. "You don't." He shook his head. "You smell like something I can't explain. Like something I want to taste every fucking inch of."

I squirmed beneath his hands because I wasn't used to being talked to like that. His words turned me on far more than I was willing to admit, but I didn't know how to handle them. I had no idea how to even begin handling him.

"We need to get back to work."

"We do." He nodded before his tongue pressed flat against the line where my jaw met my neck. The stubble along his jaw scratched against the sensitive skin, the sensation a complete contrast to the tender caress of his tongue.

My chest heaved in and out, pressing against his with every breath I attempted to take to calm myself down. It didn't help. There was nothing I could do at that moment besides take in every feeling he was giving me.

I pushed my thighs together, trying to ease the ache that had seemed to be there since he first touched me a couple of nights ago. It hadn't gone away even for a moment. I thought about it when I showered and when I tried to sleep. It was the only thing I could think about when I had pressed my fingers where his tongue had been in the darkness of my own room.

He was distracting and confusing, and that was a problem. I didn't have time for either of those things. I couldn't afford to daydream about his tongue or the way he called me baby, and I sure as heck didn't have time to wonder if I was the only one.

Did he call everyone baby when he was on his knees before them? Did he worship their bodies the way he had mine?

Those thoughts ran over and over in my head too.

Carson took too much. He always had. It didn't matter how much I would be willing to give him, he would still take more, and I didn't have any more to give him. I wasn't capable of surviving him.

I had no experience when it came to men or sex or love, but I didn't need the experience to know that.

His lips pushed against my neck, slowly and almost exploring. A kiss then a stroke of his tongue. His hands tightened against me, and I knew that if I didn't stop this now, then I wouldn't be able to bring myself to. Everything felt too good. It felt too perfect.

"Carson, we have to stop."

He groaned, the sound reverberating against my skin. I felt that one simple groan all the way to my toes.

He pressed his forehead against my shoulder, his own breathing as rapid as mine, before he pulled away from me and stared into my eyes. "You're always so responsible."

"That's a good thing."

"Is it?" He rubbed at his jaw before running his thumb over his bottom lip. "It feels really inconvenient to me."

I laughed, the small chuckle bubbling out of my throat. "That's because you're irresponsible and not used to anyone making you behave."

"True, but I think you would enjoy behaving badly with me far more than being sensible. It's a lot more fun."

I had no doubt that it was.

"I'd rather not have Mr. Sneed kicking our asses when he comes back and realizes that we haven't done anything." I leaned down and started picking up more garbage out of the yard and successfully putting a much-needed distance between us.

"All right." He shook his head before grabbing the handles of the already overflowing wheelbarrow and pushing it toward the back of the house. "I guess I'm going to have to play by your rules then."

"Exactly. Everyone needs rules."

"If you say so." He shook his head as he walked off. "I think it'd be a lot more fun if we just said fuck it and broke them, though."

CHAPTER 13
CARSON

By the time I got home from community service, I was covered in sweat and had the biggest hard-on ever. It was as if Allie had no idea what she was doing. She had been working all afternoon picking up trash and sticks and pulling weeds, but every time she bent down, I thought about the way she had looked when I was eating her from behind.

Her neck and chest glistened with sweat, and I desperately wanted to chase it all away with my tongue. She couldn't do anything without turning me on, and it made it extremely difficult to get any work done. Especially when she was adamant that there was going to be nothing else happening between us.

As soon as I walked into the house, I knew I should've gone to Beck's house instead. My parents were arguing, their voices echoing through the house as soon as I opened the door. I winced and took a deep breath. I should have been used to it by now, but the sound put me immediately on edge.

"What exactly did you think was going to happen?" My mom's voice was slurred, and I knew she had been drinking. She was almost always drinking these days. Especially on bad days.

My dad was angry and running his hands through his hair. He was rarely ever at home anymore, but when he was this was his normal.

I had become more accustomed to his anger than anything else. My dad's anger and my mother's sadness. That was what laid hidden behind these grand walls. Those were the exact things they tried to hide from everyone outside of this family.

I had no idea why they stayed together. If they thought they were benefiting me by doing so, they were completely wrong. The only benefit I got from being in this family was money. I didn't ask. I just took. My mom was either too sad or too intoxicated to notice, and my dad was typically too guilty to care.

But it was also the one thing he held over my head. It was the only power he held over me and both of us knew it. If it wasn't for his money and the life it provided me, I would never come back here.

Except for my mother.

She looked so pathetic where she stood now. She was staring up at him like he was somehow worthy of her time, and I knew that she still loved him, and deep down she hoped that he still loved her too. But he didn't.

He was nothing but a selfish prick, and every move he made seemed to drain more and more life out of her. She used to be so beautiful, so happy. But she had become a shell of who she used to be.

I hated her for it too. I knew that it wasn't her fault, but I couldn't help it.

She was my mother, and she let him break her.

But the anger I felt for her didn't touch the surface of what I felt for him. He knew exactly what he was doing. My mother loved him, and it wasn't enough.

It had never been enough for him.

It didn't matter how much she was willing to give him, and she had given him everything. She still did.

"She was at my hair salon." My mother pushed her hand against her chest. "Do you know how embarrassing that is? I was there to get my hair done, but I had to sit through looks of pity and whispers about you and your whore instead."

"Don't." My dad's voice was firm and furious, like he had some right to defend the women who he always left our home to go be with.

He couldn't defend her. She was a whore through and through.

She knew about my mom, about our family. Everyone in this town did. My dad was wealthy, and wealth in Clermont Bay was the only thing that mattered.

"Do you all need to do this tonight?" I tossed my keys onto the counter and walked to the fridge. They stared at each other as I pulled a bottle of water out.

They acted like I hadn't seen this all before. Like I didn't sit up in my bed and listen to them fight all the damn time. I was more than aware of their constant fights and my mom's constant pleas for him not to leave.

"I'm glad to see you made it home from community service." My dad turned toward me and the tone of his voice was so condescending.

"I'm glad to see you made it home from your girlfriend's

house. What's her name again?" I leaned against the counter and took a sip of my water while I stared him in the face.

"I've been at work." His hand was balled into a fist at his side. "Maybe it's time for you to start working. Then maybe you'll quit acting like a punk and actually value the money you spend."

"Yes, because work has clearly done so many good things for you."

"Carson." My mom's soft voice was a warning, but I didn't care. After everything, she still tried to defend him. Even as much as they fought, she still stuck to his side any time I said a single negative thing against him.

"What?" I looked over at her, then back at him. "I'm just pointing out the facts. He wants me to grow up and learn some values, but let me tell you, he's really been helping instill them into me."

"That's enough." My father was pissed, but I couldn't bring myself to care.

"I'm just giving you your props, Dad." I pushed off the counter because I couldn't take any more of this.

He said something behind me, but I wasn't listening to him anymore. I walked up to my mom and pressed a kiss to her cheek. Her eyes fluttered shut, and they looked so damn tired.

"I'm going to head over to Beck's for the night. Have you eaten?"

"I have." She nodded, but I wasn't sure that I believed her.

"Call me if you need me." Those were the words she should have been saying to me, but she never did.

I couldn't afford to need either of my parents. That need only led to disappointment.

Needing anyone led to nothing but disappointment.

It was why I decided a long time ago that I wasn't going to need anyone ever again. Not other than my friends, and even they were kept at a distance.

By the time I pulled back out of my driveway, all I could think about was Allie. She wouldn't know what to think if she saw my parents now. She probably had a pretty good idea. Everyone in this town thought they knew everything about everyone else's lives.

They really didn't have a clue.

But Allie had known my parents once upon a time. She had known them before everything fell apart, but there were always signs of who they would become. Of who my father was all along.

What are you doing? I sent the text before I could think better of it. I had just been with the girl a little over an hour ago, and already, I felt desperate for her again. That wasn't something I could blame on the stupid damn bet. Allie was just addicting.

I just got out of the shower.

Her reply wasn't sexual in the least bit, but I was still so turned on.

Did you think about me while you were in there?

Her next reply was instant. **Didn't we just have a talk about rules?**

This is breaking the rules too? How many rules do you have exactly? I grinned down at my phone and dropped it in my passenger seat. By the time I pulled into Beck's driveway, I had three new messages from her.

Yes. We did.

But I have lots of rules.

Especially rules about boys.

She was so damn cute. I didn't know what rules about boys she thought she had, but those rules didn't mean shit to me.

All boys or just me?

Those three little dots bounced across my screen before they disappeared, then they were back again.

Mostly you.

I grinned at her answer and sent one more message before I went inside.

Good. I look forward to breaking them.

CHAPTER 14
ALLIE

We had been showing up for our community service for over a week now, and Carson was so different each and every time. Some days he was his normal cocky self, and others he was, well, he was acting like the Carson that I used to know.

I never knew what to expect from him, and it made me so anxious.

"I don't think anyone has worked on cleaning up this yard in decades." He laid back on the front porch and spread out his arms. "Can you imagine what he's going to make us do inside the house?"

He wasn't wrong. Mr. Sneed was adamant about what he wanted us to do, and every day that we showed up, he pointed out something new.

"Do you really think he'll make us keep doing this until we have the whole dang house cleaned up?" I took a seat beside him and took a swig of my water. Fall was here, but it was still so hot outside.

"What?" He turned his head to look up at me. "Are you trying to get out of our time together already?"

"No." I shook my head, and I was being honest. I would never admit it out loud, but I actually looked forward to coming here because it forced me to be with him. More importantly, it forced him to be with me. "But I know this can't be easy for you with baseball and everything else you have going on."

"It's not." He leaned up on his elbows. "But it's not as bad as I thought."

I felt a stab of pain at his confession.

"What about you? You have to be getting ready for college and all that?" He watched me as he spoke, and I hated how he always seemed to be analyzing me.

"I am, but I just have to keep my grades up to keep my scholarship. Hopefully, it's going to cover almost all the cost of the community college."

"So, you're staying home then?" He didn't say it in a way that should make me feel ashamed, but it still did. I knew that he had far bigger plans than I did. Even without his parents' money, Carson could probably go anywhere he wanted on a baseball scholarship.

"Yeah." I nodded and swung my feet in front of me. "Have you decided where you're going to go?"

"Not officially." He sat up and reached for his water. "But I know that it's going to be far away from here."

There was another slice of pain, but I reminded myself that I didn't care. I had been going through life for the last couple of years without him, at least without this version of him, and him being gone wouldn't affect me in any way. I refused to let it. "You hate your parents that much these days?" I knew the moment the question passed my lips that I shouldn't have asked it. I knew very little of what happened with his parents and what was still happening, but I knew enough that I figured it wasn't something he wanted to talk about. Especially with me.

"Something like that." He jumped up from the porch and searched the yard. "Do you think Mr. Sneed would notice if the two of us skipped the rest of our hours today and went for a swim?"

"Yes. I do." I chuckled and stood. There was no way I was getting in trouble with Mr. Sneed again. He already looked at us like he hated us with every part of him. We didn't need to give him any other reason to hate us more.

"Okay. Then let's at least go check out the wall and see if our signatures are still there." He reached his hand out to me, and I slipped my hand in his.

He pulled me into the house, and even though it was still early afternoon and bright as could be outside, I was still freaked out as we walked through the door. We walked through the halls and over creaking floorboards until we came to the old kitchen.

Carson didn't stop as he pulled me past the old yellow stove and to the very back of the house. The sunroom was brighter than any other room in the house, but it was also creepy. Almost all of the windows were cracked or completely blown out, and I used to hate when we would come here.

But Carson dropped my hand as we entered the room, and looked up at the wall. The peeling white paint was covered in names that were scratched into the paint with pencils and markers, and some were even carved out with knives.

I stepped forward and ran my fingers over the last place Carson and I had ever signed.

Allie + Carson = BFF

It was scrawled in Carson's handwriting.

It looked so stupid now. So naïve.

"Should we sign it again?" Carson was looking over all the names on the wall, and he looked like he was remembering things just as I was.

"I don't think that's a good idea. I'm pretty sure we're going to be the one's scrubbing it off."

"Then what's it going to hurt?" Carson pulled a pen out of his pocket and flipped it between his fingers. "It wouldn't feel right if we didn't add out names one last time."

"Fine," I grumbled, and pointed to the wall.

Carson grinned and quickly signed his name dead center between names that I knew had been there for years.

"Here." He handed me the pen, and I searched the wall for somewhere to sign.

"You're not going to put your name with mine?" He looked from me to the wall.

"No. Am I supposed to?" I looked at his name where he had just written it, and it looked so different from the one before.

"It would be nice."

"But we're not even friends." I didn't mean it as an insult. It was the truth. We both knew it too.

"So?" He jerked the pen back out of my hand and went back to the spot he had just written his name. "This could be the last time we ever get to sign this wall. Don't you think we should do it together?"

He stepped back, and I couldn't help laughing at what he wrote.

Carson + Allie = enemies/friends/convicts/lovers

"We are not lovers." I pointed to the wall even though the memories of what he had done to me in this house coursed through my body and made me press my thighs together.

"We'll see." He shrugged, and as much as I tried to convince myself to tell him he was wrong, I couldn't.

CHAPTER 15
CARSON

There were so many people already there by the time we arrived at the party. I followed behind Olly, trying to push through the crowd, and even though there were plenty of people trying to get my attention, I only wanted to see her.

It was crazy.

It had barely been twenty-four hours since I had last seen her, but I felt like I was jonesing for her. It was a feeling I normally tried to stop. Usually when I thought of Allie, I shut that shit down before I allowed it to even reach the surface, but that seemed impossible these days.

"What's up?" Beck clapped his hand into mine and pulled me into a one-armed hug.

"Where are the girls?" I tried to look past him, but I didn't see them anywhere.

"Oh. I see. You're more interested in the girls now than seeing your boy?"

"I just saw you a few hours ago." I pushed against his

chest to move him out of my view. "I need to ask Frankie something."

"Oh, Frankie." He said her name so dramatically as Olly snorted. "I'm sure you're not desperate to find them because you're suddenly pussy-whipped over Allie, right?"

"I am not pussy-whipped." I stopped searching for her and looked at him to try to prove my point. "You have to be getting pussy to be whipped."

"Uh-huh." He picked up a bottle of clear liquor and started pouring it into three different cups. "You mean to tell me that all the alone time you two have been spending together has been strictly business?"

"I am."

"Nothing's happened?" Olly raised an eyebrow, and I knew he could probably see straight through me.

I didn't want to lie to them, but I also didn't want to tell them about Allie and me. I wanted us to stay in that little bubble we had created where we didn't have to discuss what was happening between us. Allie and I had been nothing for so long that I couldn't even begin to put a label on what we were doing or what we were.

She wasn't my friend, but she didn't feel like my enemy either.

She started as a bet, but nothing about what we were doing felt fake.

We felt like our past. The caress of what we used to be right at our fingertips. I knew we could never go back to that, though. Not after everything we had been through. Not after the things I had done to her body.

Allie and I would never simply be friends again.

"Nothing that you need to know about." I shrugged and prayed that he dropped it.

"So, I'm sure you're not concerned about Eli then." He poured Sprite into the three cups before situating them all in his arms.

"Why the hell would I be concerned about him?" Just hearing his name made me want to kill him, but I hadn't heard Allie talk about him at all since their date. If he was still trying to get with her, he was doing a piss-poor job at it.

"Well, right now, he's outside trying to mack on the girl who doesn't have you pussy-whipped." He winked at me before heading toward the back door. I followed him, my heart racing as we pushed through the crowd and out onto the back deck.

Olly was at my side when I spotted her. Allie was sitting on the stone steps that led down to the pool, and she was grinning up at Eli as he spoke. Josie and Frankie were both at her side, and even though Eli was a good foot from her, I still wanted to rip his head off.

"See." Beck grinned as he lifted one of the cups in his hand. "You wouldn't be concerned about that at all."

"Fuck off," I muttered and walked toward the girls with the sound of his laughter following me.

Josie was the first to see me as I made my way in front of them, and I watched as she knocked her elbow into Allie's. Allie was still grinning at Eli, nodded her head at whatever he was saying, but she broke away to look over at her friend.

I didn't give her any time to notice me. I stepped forward, taking a seat a couple stairs down from her, and I leaned back, pressing my body into the insides of her knees.

"Hey, ladies." I leaned back, looking up at all three of them just as Allie finally looked down at me.

"Hi, Carson." Frankie smiled down at me, and I knew that she knew exactly what I was doing.

Allie wasn't mine, but I was still marking my territory. She wasn't mine, but she sure as hell wasn't his.

"How's my favorite partner in crime?" I rested my arms on the top of Allie's knees, then tapped her calf.

"I'm fine." Her answer was so suspicious. If Eli wasn't watching us like a hawk, I would have laughed.

"Good." I tightened my hand around her calf and looked up at her. "I just wanted to make sure you didn't hurt yourself with me yesterday. My body was sore all over by the time we got done."

Josie's snort was loud and only fueled me further.

Allie shook her head as she stared down at me, and I knew that she was getting ready to kill me.

"We had community service together yesterday," she looked up at Eli and spoke directly to him.

"Is that what we're calling it these days?"

She slapped my shoulder. "Stop."

"Eli, what have you been up to lately?"

"Same shit as you, I suppose. School, baseball..." He shrugged and looked back to Allie.

"I don't know if I would say it's the same shit. Those things, yeah, but I've been getting myself into trouble with our girl here." I pressed against her enough to make sure she knew exactly who I was talking about. "I actually owe you a thank-you for inviting me to your date. If I hadn't been there, we would never have had our little adventure."

"No one invited you." Allie huffed, but I was too busy listening to what Eli said next.

"Well, I hate to disappoint you, but you're not invited to our next one."

I tensed at his words even though I tried not to. There was no doubt in my mind that Allie noticed. Her body stiffened behind me, but I kept the casual smile on my face as I looked at Eli with an aloofness I hoped he bought.

"Where are you taking her this time? Hooters?"

"I swear to God, you are such a dick, Carson." This came from Josie, and I smiled over my shoulder at her.

"Thank you." I pressed my hand over my heart. "I really appreciate that."

"We've actually decided not to tell anyone. That way we don't have any uninvited guests." He smirked at me like he thought he had one-upped me somehow, but this asshole didn't stand a chance.

Allie was far too good for him whether I thought so or not. She would realize that fact soon enough for herself.

"That's smart. I'd hate for her to leave your date with another guy again."

He puffed out his chest and stood to his full height. "She's not going to be leaving with anyone but me."

Good. I was pissing him off.

Allie pushed against my back and tightened her knees around me. "You all know that I'm right here, right? Neither one of you speak for me."

"You're right." Eli was so damn quick to back down, but I wouldn't.

She could be pissed at me if she wanted to. I couldn't just sit here and let him talk about her like she was somehow his. She would never be his.

"It's too bad you're going to be gone for fall break too. You're going to miss one hell of a camping trip." It was only a couple of weeks away, and it would be his last chance to do anything with her.

Then it would be the end of their stupid damn bet, and he would leave her the hell alone. That was what I had to tell myself. The way he was staring at her right now had to be because of the bet.

But he was a damn good actor because he was looking at her like he actually cared. He ran his hand over his jaw and stared down at her like she was his girl.

"Here, Allie." Beck passed her one of the cups I saw him making before taking a seat beside me.

"What's up, Eli?"

Eli didn't answer him. He was still staring at her. "Allie, are you going?"

"To the senior camping trip? I-I think so?" She nodded even though her answer was so unsure. "Everyone's going."

"I'll be there." I winked at him. Everyone would. All Clermont High and Prep seniors did the camping trip every year. It was tradition. "Don't worry. I won't let her get eaten by a bear or anything."

"Such a gentleman." He crossed his arms. "At least that's what I've always heard. Carson, the honorable. I'm still trying to understand how you manage to get all those girls to sleep with you when you're so fucked up you won't even kiss them on the mouth." He chuckled, and I tensed. "Is it a mommy issue or a daddy one? I know you have both."

I was on my feet before I could think rationally about what I was doing. My chest hit his, and there was a spark of fear in his eyes. He had plenty of words to throw at me, but this asshole was nothing more than talk.

"You'd be surprised to find out how little a girl needs you to kiss her mouth when you eat her pussy like it was fucking made for you. Maybe you can ask for Allie's opinion on it when you have your little date."

There was a shocked inhale behind me, but I didn't budge. I knew that I would regret what I said later, but the urge to stake my claim on Allie flowed through every part of me.

And the shock in Eli's eyes was worth every single consequence I would have to pay.

"You motherfucker." Eli raised his hands and shoved against my chest. I stumbled back a step, but I was back on him just as quickly.

I swung my fist, connecting with his jaw, and pain sliced through my knuckles at the feel of his bone beneath them. Blood dripped down his chin as he lunged for me. He wrapped his arms around my middle, and we both fell backward from his weight.

My back hit the ground, taking both of our weight, and I groaned. But I didn't have time to think about the pain. Eli was swinging his fists in my direction, and I blocked his first hit before the second landed half on my nose and half on my mouth.

My vision blacked out for a second, but I was already throwing my elbow into his head and knocking him off of me. I slammed my fist into the side of his face before gripping his shirt in my opposite hand and bringing him closer to me. He tried to fight me off, but I felt out of control.

I wanted to kill him. Every bit of pain, every damn thing he said, fueled me and I couldn't see anything other than my hatred for him.

It didn't matter that there was screaming around us, or that I could hear my name being yelled somewhere in the back of my head. Eli gripped my arm, trying to push me off of him, but he was too weak.

I lifted my fist, ready to pummel his ass again, but arms wrapped around me from behind. My arms were forced into my sides, and I was jerked off Eli and to my feet. I tried to fight against it, but then Olly's voice was in my ear.

"Calm the fuck down."

Eli charged toward me before one of his boys blocked his path, and I tried to yank out of Olly's hold to get my hands on him. But then Beck was in front of me. He pushed on my chest to help Olly back me away from that asshole, and I didn't fight them.

"I'm good." I shook them off and stretched out my hands.

Everything from the last few moments raced through my mind. There was still chaos going on around us. A scurry of activity, laughter, people freaking out, but I searched through it all for Allie.

"Where's Allie?" I wiped at my nose and brought my hand out to look at the blood that I collected.

"I think it's time we get out of here." Beck scratched at the back of his head. "The girls will get Allie."

I wasn't leaving without her. I wasn't walking out of here and leaving her with him.

"Fuck that." I noticed so many faces I knew, but none of them were her. I pushed past Beck, but he gripped my arm before I could get too far.

"This isn't a good idea. Especially after the things you just said. We need to go."

Because I hadn't just said what I said about eating Allie in front of Eli. I had said it to anyone who was listening. I had acted like she was as disposable as anyone else, but she wasn't.

But I had treated her that way.

I looked over toward Eli, and that was where I found her. She was standing in front of him, and she looked as disheveled as I knew I did. One of her hands was tucked into her back pocket and the other bounced against her thigh.

I stepped toward her, but Beck stopped me again. "Man, come on. I think you've done enough for tonight."

"Fuck that." I jerked my arm from his grip. "I need to talk to her."

He shook his head, and I knew that he thought this was a horrible idea. But I was still making my way toward her.

"Allie," I called for her, and she startled before turning in my direction.

"Don't." She was still several feet away from me, but she still took a step back. "Do not come anywhere near me, Carson."

Eli stepped behind her, and I saw red.

"Seriously?" I pointed at that motherfucker. "You have a fucking death wish, don't you?"

"Stop!" Allie turned into him, and my chest felt like it was caving in on itself.

"You're seriously picking his side?" I couldn't fucking believe her.

"I'm not picking anyone's side. I'm not some sort of damn game piece you two can use any way you want."

"Allie, just let me talk to you." I stepped closer to her but stopped when I saw her wince.

"What exactly would you like to talk about, Carson?" She held up her hands. "You didn't mind sharing my fucking business a few minutes ago so what's the issue now?"

"I shouldn't have said that."

"No shit." She was pissed. Allie rarely ever cursed, and she wrinkled her nose in this adorable way that I shouldn't have even noticed. "But that's what you do, isn't it? Don't treat me like an idiot. I know exactly who you are."

She turned away from me, and Eli wrapped his hand around the inside of her elbow.

"Don't leave with him." The plea left my lips, and everyone heard it.

She heard it too. She paused and took a moment before she turned to face me again. "Who should I leave with then?" There wasn't an ounce of hesitation in her voice. "You just made it perfectly clear that the only thing that has ever happened between you and me is that you ate me out."

"Oh shit."

I had no idea who said that, but I didn't care.

"Is there someone else you'd prefer me to go with?"

"Me." I stumbled over the word. "Just let me take you home."

"No." She shook her head and started backing away. "I think you've done enough for one night."

Then she walked away with Eli trailing behind her, and there wasn't a damn thing I could do.

CHAPTER 16

ALLIE

I had never been so angry while getting ready for a date before.

To be fair, I didn't have much experience at all, but I didn't think many girls almost ripped their hair out while they were brushing it or had to reapply their lipstick three different times because they were so irritated.

I should have canceled.

If I wasn't so worried about what Carson thought, I would have, but I refused to let his pissing contest ruin everything. I was more than aware that both Carson and Eli had been acting like douchebags, but I wasn't nearly as bothered by Eli.

I didn't know if it was because he didn't say the things that Carson said or if it was because Carson meant more to me than he ever would. I prayed it was the first because the second reason made me irrationally angry.

It made me want to go on this date and have the best night of my life. I wanted to prove to Carson that he wasn't the only one who could do what they wanted with whomever they wanted. I was desperate to show him that I wasn't just some girl who he could do with as he pleased then pretend like she didn't matter.

I didn't need Carson Hale.

Despite what he thought, I was more than capable of finding someone else that was interested in me.

When he had told Eli to ask me for my opinion on whether or not I needed him to kiss me after he had finished kissing me between my thighs, I wanted to kill him. And of course, part of that was because I was mortified by what he said in front of everyone, but the bigger part was because I did need him to kiss me.

I had been thinking about it constantly.

The idea that I could be just like any other girl to Carson never truly crossed my mind. Even when he was cruel to me, I knew he did so because I had meant something to him. He hadn't hated me for no reason. He hated me because I had meant something to him and I had let him down.

I hurt him, and he used that hurt to fuel his anger for me. An anger that I had become accustomed to, but then it changed. Or at least I thought it had.

But Carson's cruelty was just morphing into something new. He didn't need hurtful words or bored glances. He was going to break me, and I was going to let him.

Because I had always been an idiot when it came to him.

I had always cared about him to my own detriment, but I couldn't fix Carson. I couldn't even help him. He was messed up and angry, and he would always keep me far enough away that I couldn't see the truth he was always trying to hide.

And I was done with trying.

If this was the guy he wanted to be, then he could be

him, but I was done playing his games. I wasn't going to be his doormat or punching bag or the girl he pretended to like when we were alone.

He made it perfectly clear last night where we stood, and there would be no more confusion on my part. It didn't matter what it had been like over the last couple weeks. Nothing mattered except the truth.

Carson didn't want me. He just refused to let anyone else have me.

He refused to let me be happy.

By the time I pulled up to the putt-putt course, I was already worked up and irritable again just from thinking about him.

Forget him, Allie.

Tonight wasn't about Carson. It was about having fun and letting my past become my past.

Eli stood near the entrance as I walked up, and he looked handsome despite the swollen split lip he was sporting. I knew Carson probably looked about the same. It served them both right for acting like complete and total idiots.

"You look beautiful." Eli grinned and pulled me into a hug. I tensed at the contact but reminded myself to calm down.

This was what I wanted. A nice guy who actually gave a shit. A guy who actually wanted to be with me.

"Thank you. You look nice as well." I pulled out of his touch and pushed my hair behind my ear as I looked toward the entrance. "Are you ready to play?"

"Yes. Let's do this." He reached his hand out for mine, and I let him take it.

We walked hand in hand inside, and he didn't drop it

until he had to take out his wallet to pay. Then he grabbed my hand again as we got our golf clubs and balls.

"I'm so happy you decided to come out tonight." He smiled down at me, and I knew he was remembering last night. I was so upset after I walked away from Carson, so ready to just go home and wallow in my pity, but Eli had asked me to come out with him today.

He told me he wanted to make up for being an ass, for saying anything to Carson that caused the fight. I knew that he probably wasn't really sorry, and I didn't forgive him for the things he said about Carson's family. But I couldn't just sit at my house and think about him nonstop.

It wasn't healthy.

So here I was.

"Me too." I dropped his hand and tested my golf club. "I've never actually done this before, so it could be dangerous."

He chuckled and placed his ball on the ground to take his first shot. "I don't think I've ever seen anyone get injured in a game of putt-putt before."

"You never know." I shrugged. "I've been hurt doing simpler tasks."

"Are you telling me that you're a klutz?" He took his shot, and it went directly in the hole.

"Maybe a little bit. One time, I cut my hand wide open while trying to climb a tree. We had no idea what I even managed to cut it on, but I almost passed out from just looking at the cut." I smiled, but then remembered that Carson was the one who was with me that day. He was also the one who bandaged my hand up so much that it looked like it had been amputated.

My mom freaked when we walked back into my house,

but the cut she found underneath was nothing compared to the bandaging.

"Okay. So, don't let you climb the windmill on hole nine and don't yell for you in a medical emergency. Got it." He grinned and put my ball on the ground where his had just been. "Anything else I should know about you before I get too involved?"

I knew he was just playing around, but I wanted to tell him that there was. I felt the need to tell him that even though I was here with him, I couldn't stop thinking about someone else.

"No." I shook my head. "At least not yet. I don't give away all the juicy details on the first date."

"This is technically our second."

"Oh, yeah. Right." I tried to laugh off my blunder. "I'll at least give it until date five before I tell you whether or not I'm a serial killer or if I collect clowns or anything like that."

"You don't think those are details I should have now?" He was smiling and playing along with my banter, and it felt so normal. This was what a date should be like. Two people talking and joking and getting to know each other.

But it also felt so incredibly boring.

"Nope." I swung my club and hit the red ball. It soared down the course, faster than I expected, but it didn't go anywhere near the hole I was supposed to be aiming for. "If I give away too many of those spicy details now, then I might lose my allure."

"I highly doubt that." His gaze fell to my lips. "I'm pretty sure there is nothing you could say that would make you any less captivating."

I could feel the heat crawling up my chest, and I knew

my cheeks were probably reddening. "That's very sweet, but I think I may have you fooled."

"We'll see." He walked to the end of the hole and pointed to my ball. "Come on. I'll help line you up and show you how to hit this thing."

I moved to stand in front of him, and he wrapped his arms around me to grip the club over my hands.

"You have to look at the hole and visualize the ball going in. Think about the exact place and speed you need to hit on the ball to make the trajectory aim straight for our target."

I was barely listening to a thing he said because I couldn't honestly care less about hitting that dang ball in, but his body was warm against my back and his arms felt good around me. I tried to relax as he moved our arms back and forth up to the ball. He was so focused on the game, and I was trying to focus on nothing but him.

He swung our arms forward until the club connected with the ball, and it did exactly what he said. The ball rolled along the turf and dropped directly into the hole.

"I did it." I cheered, and he chuckled behind me.

"I had absolutely nothing to do with that, right?"

"Not a thing." I spun around to face him, and the smell of his cologne was warm and expensive. "I just needed a warm-up shot."

"Uh-huh." He grinned down at me, and I suddenly wished he would kiss me. And guilt felt like it would eat me alive. I didn't feel guilty over Carson, God only knew who the heck he was with, but I felt guilty because I wanted Eli to kiss me simply because Carson wouldn't.

Eli was right here in front of me. He was handsome and kind, and I was desperate for him to kiss me because I wanted to prove something that I couldn't even explain.

"Are you saying that you think I'm bad?"

"No." He lifted his hand and tucked a few strands of my hair behind my ear.

I geared myself up as he touched me, waiting for the spark of energy to shoot through my body, that deep pull of desire, but it didn't come. His fingers skimmed down my jaw, and it was nice. My heart still raced thinking about him kissing me, but it was different.

"I'm simply saying that maybe you're not as good as you think you are. My instructions were probably pretty invaluable."

"Maybe." I shrugged and moved the smallest fraction closer to him. "But maybe it was just the two of us together. Teamwork and all that."

"Yeah?" His grin deepened and a small dimple showed on his right cheek. "You think the two of us make a good team?"

"I think so." I wrapped my arm around the back of his neck and my stomach fluttered. I was normally not this forward. "But I think we need a little more research to find out."

"Agreed." He leaned forward and it was only a second later that his lips finally met mine.

They were soft yet firm, and I tightened my hand around his neck to pull him closer. I wanted more. I wanted to feel more, to crave more. I just needed more.

He took the hint, sliding his tongue against the seam of my lips, and I opened instantly for him. His tongue touched mine before slipping into my mouth, and I moaned at the contact. Eli pushed his fingers into my hair, and he tightened them as he deepened the kiss.

It was nice.

The feel of his hand, the taste of him, the way he kissed me. All of it was so nice.

But I had felt more desire when Carson had simply leaned against my legs the night before and that pissed me off.

I deepened the kiss, my tongue chasing his, and he pulled me tighter against him. His stomach pressed against mine, and I could feel how turned on he was. I tried to hold on to that thought. I was turning Eli Scott on. He could have almost any girl he wanted, but he was here with me, and he wanted me.

He pulled away slightly, his lips still pressing gently against mine, as he tried to catch his breath. "I'd say we work pretty well together." He chuckled, the sound breathy and rough.

"Absolutely." I nodded and tried to convince myself that this was what I wanted.

He took a step back, putting some space between us, and grabbed his club. He reached for my hand, and I let him take it. Eli was the kind of guy I was supposed to date. He was exactly what I should want.

But I couldn't stop the deep, aching feeling at the pit of my stomach.

Eli was the guy I needed, but he wasn't the one I wanted.

CHAPTER 17

CARSON

I showed up to community service almost an hour early.

Don't ask me why. I just couldn't stand sitting in my house and staring at the walls while thoughts raced through my head. Frankie had told me that Allie went on a date with Eli yesterday. She went on a date with him, but she refused to even answer my calls or my text.

I needed to give her space. That was Frankie's suggestion, but space had never worked with Allie and me. The last time we put space between the two of us, I turned her into my enemy.

Now, when this was supposed to be nothing more than a damn bet, I was going to make her worse than that. She was going to hate me.

I knew that the moment I had agreed to this stupid fucking bet, but I hadn't really cared then. She already hated me, and I didn't give a shit what she thought. I had forced myself to stop giving a shit.

But she fucked with my head.

I started this to keep her away from Eli and Lucas and all

their fucking boys, but now I wanted to hide her away and never let a single one of them touch her.

That was all I could think about after Frankie told me the news about their date. She was pissed as hell at me over the fight and the things that I said, and I understood that. But Eli wasn't a saint. He was just as guilty as I was, but instead of being mad at him, she had decided to go on another date with him.

Then I saw the picture he posted on his Instagram.

It was innocent enough. They were standing together in front of a fake windmill at the putt-putt course, but she was smiling like she was having the best time of her life. I was at home trying to think of every possible scenario where I could convince her to forgive me, and she was smiling up at him like she had never been happier.

I had thrown my phone so hard at the wall that my screen shattered into a thousand pieces, but I didn't care. I felt so out of control, and I didn't know how to fix it.

The solution was simple. I needed to walk away.

I did what I should have. I told Allie about Eli. I tried to warn her away, but she hadn't listened. She didn't want to hear what I said.

And now she was choosing him over me, and I should let her.

When she got hurt, I could simply say 'I told you so' and walk away with a guilt-free conscience, but I couldn't.

That pissed me off more than anything.

I shoved the lawnmower over the overgrown grass and cursed. This damn thing was not made for grass that hadn't been cut in probably ten years, and it kept getting bogged down every few minutes. It was like it knew that I was already pissed off and wanted to contribute to the cause.

"I swear to God." I pushed it over an especially thick patch of grass and kept going. I already finished mowing the entire front of the house, and it almost looked like a different place.

The damn mower got stuck again, and I shut it off before I kicked it. I took a deep breath and ran my t-shirt over my face to wipe away the sweat. It was still relatively early, but the heat was already wearing me down.

Mr. Sneed had been shocked when I had arrived here so early on a Sunday morning. I didn't know if he had set up security cameras or maybe an alarm system, but he walked up to the gate within minutes of me arriving.

He was grumpy as ever, and he barely spoke two words as he let me in through the gate, then left the way he came. I preferred it that way anyway.

I turned toward the front of the house, in search of my water bottle I had left there, and stopped in my tracks when I noticed Allie leaning against the side of the house. She had her legs crossed in front of her, and she was clearly watching me.

"When did you get here?" I walked past her, and she followed me.

"A few minutes ago. I was going to let you know I was here, but I figured I'd let you and your lawnmower get your fight out of the way before I did."

"Funny." I picked up my bottle and unscrewed the cap with far too much force. I needed to calm down. I should have been the one apologizing right now, but I was so damn pissed that I couldn't find the words to do it.

She watched me as I took a deep drink of my water and put it back on the porch.

"I'm going to get back to it then. You can watch if you

want, or Mr. Sneed left some paint scrapers over there." I pointed to the front steps. "He wants us to get rid of the chipping paint on the porch."

"Okay." She stared at me with her arms crossed over her chest. "Is that all you're really going to say to me?"

"What exactly would you like me to say?"

I should have been saying that I was sorry. I should have been begging for her forgiveness, but I was too damn angry right now. I knew that I would just say the wrong thing and make her even more pissed off than she already was.

I just needed to walk away, give us both space, and focus on the task at hand.

"How was your date?" That was the exact opposite of what I should have been saying.

Her face reddened almost instantly. "How did you even know that I went on a date?"

"Well, Eli's Instagram post of the two of you didn't really keep it a secret. You two looked like you had a good time."

"We did." She huffed and stared at me. "Am I not allowed to have a good time with him? Is that one of the rules of being a girl you go down on but don't kiss?"

I shook my head because she had only been here for a few minutes and already she was getting under my skin. "I told you that night that I was sorry. If you had answered my calls or text, I would have told you then too."

"You can tell me now."

I stared at her, and she was so damn beautiful. Her chest rose and fell so quickly, and I knew that she was getting as angry as I was. "I'm sorry, okay?"

I held out my arms and stepped back. I needed to get back to work. This conversation wasn't going to be good for either of us.

"I shouldn't have said that, and I'm sorry. Eli got under my skin, and I shouldn't have let him. I really do hope that you had a great date." I turned away from her but stopped as soon as she spoke.

"You're such an ass."

"I just said I was sorry. How does that make me an ass?"

"Because you don't mean it. You're not sorry for what you said, and you don't wish I had a good date. I don't know what you want from me." Her fingers messed with the bottom of her t-shirt as she looked away, then brought her gaze back to mine. "What's so wrong with Eli? Why do you hate him so much?"

"Because he's a douchebag." The answer was pretty obvious to me.

"No. He's not."

"Okay, Allie. You barely even know the guy, but sure, we'll go on your opinion of him."

"My opinion is the only one that matters when it comes to who I want to date, Carson." She pointed at her chest as she spoke. "You always tell me there's something wrong with anyone who shows the least bit of interest in me."

"No. I don't."

"Yes. You do!" she yelled and moved toward me. "I know that I hurt you when we were younger, but I didn't know. I had no clue what was happening with your parents or I wouldn't have gone out with that stupid guy. I would have answered your calls."

My chest ached because it really had nothing and everything to do with that. It wasn't just that she wasn't there when I needed her. It was the fact that I needed her at all. I saw what happened to my mother when she needed my father. I never wanted to become that. I refused to give anyone that kind of power over me.

"It doesn't matter, Allie." I laughed and tried to play it off. "I was trying to spare you from getting your heart broken by some asshole. That's all. But do whatever you want. I won't stand in your way."

"You are such a damn coward." Her hands were balled into fists at her sides.

"Me not wanting you to get hurt makes me a coward?" I shook my head and looked down at her.

"You using that as your excuse makes you a coward." She stepped even closer to me, and I could easily reach out and touch her. "You just don't want me to be happy."

Her gaze searched mine, and there was so much hurt there. So many things hidden that neither one of us was willing to say. She shook her head, clearly disappointed in me, and turned to walk away.

I should have let her.

I should have stopped what we were doing right here and now, but I couldn't. I caught her arm in my hand before she could get too far, and I tried to catch my breath as my mind raced with what to say.

"I want you to be happy."

Allie laughed without an ounce of humor and looked away from me.

"Just not with him."

She turned back to me, and she looked even angrier than before. "That's not fair, Carson. It's not up to you who I do or don't date."

"I know that." My fingers tightened around her arm almost involuntarily. I didn't want her to leave. I didn't know what I would do if she walked away right now. "I just…" I didn't know what to say.

"You what, Carson? For once, just tell me the truth. What do you want?"

"You." I finally dropped her arm and took a step back. "Is that what you want to hear? I want you, but I can't have you. I want you, and I'm insanely fucking jealous that Eli Scott gets to parade you around under my nose."

"Why can't you have me?" She barely whispered her question, and I hated how broken she sounded. This was what I was doing to her. This is exactly what we would become.

"Because." I ran my hand through my hair. "I don't do the whole girlfriend thing. It's just not in the cards for me."

"That's such a bullshit answer." She shook her head. "What are you so afraid of?"

I chuckled and smiled down at her. Everything inside me begged for me to get away, from this situation, this talk, from her. She was the thing I wanted most in this world, but she was also the one thing I couldn't have.

"I'm not afraid of anything. I'm just not capable of giving you the things that I know you would want, and you're not capable of only having the things I'm willing to give."

And I'm not willing to break your heart.

I wished I could just say that out loud. That I never wanted her to become like my mother, and that more than anything, I feared I was more like my father than I would ever be willing to admit.

"So, what?" There were tears in her eyes when she looked back up at me, and I forced myself not to react.

This was how I should have left it from the beginning. I should have never gotten involved in the first place.

"We'll just go back to hating each other and pretending like the other one doesn't exist."

"If that's what you want." I shrugged my shoulders. "But surely we can be friendly with each other. After all, we do have a criminal record together now."

"Right." She stepped back, and I could almost see her shutting her walls down around her. "I'm going to get to work before Mr. Sneed comes back and yells at us."

"Okay. Yeah. He wasn't very happy when he let me in this morning." I started to walk away from her, and it felt wrong. Everything about this conversation, about the way we were leaving things, about me walking away from her.

But it was the only choice I had.

CHAPTER 18
ALLIE

"I swear that I would have been fine if you all just left me at home," I grumbled, and pulled my bag out of the back of Beck's SUV. "There's still time for me to go back. I'll hitch a ride."

"Not happening." Josie shoved another bag into my hands as she unloaded. "You're not missing the senior camping trip just because Carson's a jerk."

"Honestly, you should really be used to it by now," Beck chimed in from where he was getting the tents down from the top of the car.

"Yeah. That's not a real thing." Frankie knocked her elbow into my side. "You shouldn't have to get used to a guy being a jerk, but we're just going to ignore him. I'm not even supposed to be here since I'm not a senior, so you and I will lay low."

"Fine, but I'm also going to be super pissed if I get eaten by a bear out here."

"There are too many people here." Josie loaded her arms, then Frankie and I followed her to the campsite where tons of other students were already setting up. "I know there is at least one person here who is slower than us."

"So, we're just going to sacrifice them?" Frankie laughed.

"Exactly. Maybe we can even knock Carson over and let the bear get his dumb ass."

"Okay. This trip is sounding better and better." I chuckled and put my bags on the ground. "A little relaxation. Possibly get rid of the boy who's bound and determined to break my heart."

"Who's breaking your heart?" I heard Carson's voice before I saw him, and I tensed. "Am I going to have to kick someone's ass already?"

"No. Thank you. If you want to do something useful, help Beck set up our tents." Josie deflected his question, and I avoided looking at him.

"Is this where we're setting everything up?" He set his own bags down next to me, and I wished he wouldn't.

Part of me wished we didn't have any mutual friends, so I didn't have to see him at all. That would make my life a lot easier.

Because I had been avoiding him ever since our conversation after my date with Eli. He went back to acting like nothing had ever happened so easily. He grinned and smirked and did the job at Mr. Sneed's like he wasn't affected at all.

But I was.

I could barely stand to be around him. I wanted to scream at him, hit him, do anything to make him stop acting like he was so unaffected by everything. This was the version of Carson I hated. Not the cruel one or the flirty one.

It was this Carson who didn't care about anything.

My mind raced with thought after thought and my heart

felt like it was going to beat out of my chest every time I was around him, but he just smiled and went about his day like nothing had happened.

It was driving me crazy. I couldn't stand it. Especially not when we were alone at Mr. Sneed's. It had gotten so bad that I had asked Mr. Sneed if I could do a project in the house just so I could avoid him. I went into that stuffy, dirty, haunted house and worked on knocking down cobwebs with a broom so I wouldn't have to be beside him while he dug out the flowerbeds at the front of the house.

Carson had looked at me like I was crazy when I asked, but I didn't care what he thought.

He made it clear where we stood, and I had to force myself not to care.

"Yes." Frankie wrapped her arm in Carson's and pulled him toward the edge of the campsite we were at. "But your tent is going down here on the end near mine. I need you to be the first line of defense against bears."

"There aren't any bears out here." He chuckled but let her pull him along.

"I hear what you're saying, but I don't believe you. I'd rather not take any chances."

"You okay?" Josie whispered, and I pulled my gaze away from watching Carson walk away with Frankie to look at her.

"Yes. Of course." I smiled and looked around the site. "I think I'm going to put my tent on this end." I pointed to the spot that would be the farthest from Carson's, even though there still wouldn't be a ton of room between us with the way the campsite curved.

"I think that's a good idea." Josie smiled and pulled out a tarp from one of her bags. "That way you're my first line of defense against bears."

I laughed and rolled my eyes. "You better be careful. My chicken ass might end up in the tent with you and Beck."

"Not happening." Beck dropped everything he was holding at our feet and wiped at his brow. "I need alone time with my girl."

"She literally lives with you, and you both have the pool house all to yourselves." I pointed out the obvious.

"Yeah, but I also have a little sister who bestied up with my girl. She never leaves."

Josie smacked him in the stomach, and he groaned. "Be nice."

"I am." He held up his hands to keep her from hitting him again. "I'm just making sure it's clear that no one is coming in that tent besides me and you."

"No. It's fine." I pulled my tent out of the pile at his feet and started unzipping it. "I see how it is. After all the times I defended you so you could get your girl, you're not willing to defend me in an animal attack."

Beck rolled his eyes, and I was one hundred percent sure he was going to be completely over us before the trip ended. "We'll put our tent right next to yours, and I'll give you a code word. If I hear you yell it, I will defend you with my life."

"But then I'll have to listen to you two getting it on all night." I wrinkled my nose. I loved them both, but I didn't want to stay awake all night trying to figure out if every noise I heard was a bear or Beck.

"That's the price you're going to have to pay for my protection." Beck shrugged like he had just given me the best deal ever.

"I'll put my tent next to yours." Olly walked up with a backpack on his back and a bunch of things in his hands that I didn't even know what they were used for. "If you get too scared, you can bunk with me."

"Deal." I stuck out my hand and he shook it with a smile on his face.

I had no idea why I hadn't fallen for a guy like him. Olly was incredible and sweet, and if I wasn't so stupidly into his best friend and my best friend wasn't secretly into him, I would jump on the chance.

But I would never do that to Frankie.

We spent the next hour or so putting up our tents and setting up our campsite. There were already so many people here from both Prep and Clermont High, and I realized that I could do this. There were enough people around that I could easily avoid Carson.

By the time I sat down next to the fire Olly had just built, Carson was nowhere to be found.

"I'm going to sleep, so good tonight." Frankie sighed as she took the seat next to me. "I'm already so worn out."

"Nope." Josie plopped down in her lap and looked back and forth between the both of us. "No one is going to bed early tonight or hiding out in their tents. We're drinking."

"I don't think that's a very good idea for me." I held my fingers out toward the fire to warm them. I had expected it to be hot, but as soon as the sun started to fall the crisp, cool evening air moved in.

"It's a great idea." Josie was trying to be convincing, but she wasn't. "None of us have to drive home. If anyone gets out of hand, we can put you straight into your tent, and you need to let loose a little."

"She's right," Frankie said before yawning. "We can play some drinking games, find you and me some guys to flirt with" —she winked at me— "then we can fall into our sleeping bags and do it all again tomorrow."

"Exactly!" Josie grabbed my hand in hers and pouted. "Come on, Allie. They are setting up flip cup as we speak."

I looked between the two of them, and I knew that there was no way I was going to tell them no. "If I get sloppy, you put my ass to bed."

"Done." Josie jumped up and pulled Frankie and me from our seats. We followed her to the center of the camp where most of the students were congregating, and I tried not to look around for Carson.

Josie grabbed all three of us a beer from the cooler Beck was sitting on, and she kissed his cheek before turning back to us. "Here we go." She handed us both a beer, and I quickly opened the tab and took a sip.

"Now, do we see any prospective gentlemen? Anyone who tickles your fancy?"

As soon as she said it, my eyes landed on Carson. He was sitting on top of one of the picnic tables with a joint pressed to his lips and a group of girls vying for his attention. I didn't recognize the guy he was talking to, but I recognized a handful of the girls. One of them was the girl he took on his date with me and Eli.

But he didn't seem to be paying her a single bit of attention.

"Nope." I shook my head and forced myself to look away from him. "But didn't you say something about drinking games."

"I did." She grinned and locked her arm in mine. "Let's go."

We walked up to the table that was nearest Carson, and I turned my back to avoid looking at him. The table was currently being set up for a game of flip cup, and Josie pushed all three of us into the game before anyone could object.

Two of the guys on our team played baseball with the guys, but for the life of me, I couldn't remember their names.

"The team that loses all have to take a shot," the guy at the head of the table yelled out with his hand in the air. "Ready, set, go!" He brought his hand down, and Frankie lifted her cup to her mouth and swallowed down the alcohol before setting her cup back on the table.

It took a few times to get her cup flipped over, but we were already in the lead. Josie was next, and it took her a few more tries than Frankie.

"Come on, Josie," one of the guys yelled, and I couldn't help laughing when she got so frustrated with the cup.

"There!" She finally landed it, then knocked her arm into mine.

I grabbed my cup, quickly drinking the cold beer in a couple gulps, then I set the cup back onto the table and flipped it with my finger. To my amazement, it landed upright the first time, and cheering broke out around me as the guy to my left raced to drink his.

The laughter and competitiveness of those around me was infectious, and I found myself getting into the game without even thinking about it. It was the last guy's turn to go, and he was neck and neck with the player on the other team.

Josie was telling him to go beside me, and we all screamed when his cup finally landed upright only seconds before the other team.

We all jumped up and down, and you would have thought we had just won the Olympic Games. But I didn't care. I wrapped my arms around my friends, and all three of us laughed as we celebrated.

"Does that mean this table is open for a new opponent?"

I looked up at Eli, where he stood across the table directly in front of me, and he was grinning like I was the best thing he had ever seen.

"What are you doing here?" I hadn't expected him to be here. The last time we spoke, he was getting ready to leave with his family for his fall break.

"I talked my parents into letting me stay home." He looked so handsome even though he was just wearing a hoodie and a pair of gym shorts. It was in the way he was looking at me, the way he smiled at me. "Have you already put your tent up?"

Josie knocked her hand against mine as he asked the question, but I ignored her.

"I have. It's over there." I pointed to our site.

"Mind if I put my bag down there for now?"

I could feel my friends watching me, and I didn't know if it was that or the thought of him staying in my tent with me that made my heart suddenly race.

"No." I shook my head and walked toward him. "I'll show you which one is mine."

CHAPTER 19

CARSON

I watched Allie walk away with Eli over an hour ago, and I was ready to kill something.

He wasn't supposed to be here.

If I had known that he was going to be here, I would have... I don't know, but I would have done something differently.

But everything I had done up until this moment had pushed her directly into his arms. I had hurt her. I knew that before I ever saw the look on her face.

The fact that she had been completely ignoring me since our talk only sealed that fact. Allie hated me, and any chance I stood with her was ruined. But I wasn't looking for a chance. I just didn't want her to give it to him. Not with everything I knew.

Even if he really liked Allie and wasn't just doing all this for that stupid fucking bet, I wouldn't want him anywhere near her.

"What's he doing here?" I nodded my head in the direction of him and Allie as I walked up to our campsite. They were sitting side by side, and she was laughing at something he was showing her on his phone.

"What does it matter?" Josie cocked her head to the side and watched me from where she sat. "Allie told us what you said to her. If you're not interested in being with her, then leave her alone."

"This has nothing to do with whether or not I'm interested in being with her. Eli is not a good guy." I took the empty seat next to her which I was sure was meant for Beck. Allie didn't look up. She hadn't noticed my presence at all.

"And you are?"

Frankie winced at Josie's question, but she didn't offer a word to defend me. Not that I blamed her.

"No. I'm not." I shook my head but didn't take my eyes off Allie. "Which is exactly why I'm not interested in dating your friend, but you all can't seriously think that he's good for her."

"I think that Allie deserves to have fun on this trip without you trying to ruin it for her." Josie shrugged like that was the simplest explanation ever. "Do I think that Eli is her one true love? No. Do I think that maybe she can have fun with him for a little while and forget about you? Absolutely."

"And what about you?" I looked over at Frankie.

"I think you just need to give her some space. I don't think either one of you are thinking very clearly right now."

"Okay, fine." I held up my hands. "I will give her space and let her do whatever it is that she wants, but do not come crying to me when he hurts her."

My heart raced and my chest ached, and I felt like I was going to be sick. The last thing I wanted to do was give her space, and even though I just told them I would, I knew that there was a very slim chance that I would be able to stay away from her.

Even now, just looking at her sitting there wearing his baseball hoodie, I wanted to rip it from her body and demand she wear mine instead. I knew how insane that thought was.

I couldn't have it both ways. I couldn't keep Allie at a distance while simultaneously keeping her away from every other guy who could possibly be interested in her. And that was what this had become. I had told myself that I just wanted to keep her away from Eli because of the bet, but really, I couldn't imagine her with anyone.

Especially not now that I knew she was a virgin.

I used to tell myself that it didn't matter what she was doing. I figured when I didn't see her that she had to be off with some other guy.

Because Allie was fucking gorgeous.

She was gorgeous and sweet, and she was so damn different than any other girl I had ever met. I couldn't imagine how she had gone through high school without every single guy she met falling head over heels for her.

And maybe they did. Maybe Allie just wasn't interested. That was the only thing that made sense.

"If he hurts her, I'll kill him myself." Josie followed my gaze. "But I doubt she'll even let him get close enough to do so."

I nodded my head because she was probably right, but I would be the one to kill him when he hurt her. I had warned the motherfucker, and he didn't listen. Anything that happened beyond that point was on him.

He thought he was going to beat me in some stupid bet, in this stupid game they were playing, but I didn't have time for their fucking games. Not with Eli and definitely not with Lucas. I knew that he was as much a part of it as anyone, because that asshole did nothing without a reason.

Even tonight, I knew that he was here. I had spotted him on the opposite side of the site with the rest of his douchebag friends. The only one missing was Eli, and of course, he was stuck right under my fucking nose.

There was no way I was going to be able to sit there and watch them together all night. Especially not after the shit he said to me only a few days ago.

And the things I said to her were even worse.

It didn't matter if that was what she actually wanted, I couldn't stand to watch it. I didn't think that I could watch her with anyone.

"What are we going to do for the rest of the night?" I turned to the girls and smiled.

"It's already midnight." Frankie laughed before covering her yawn.

"So? Let's go skinny-dipping."

"There is no way in hell." Josie shook her head. "It's freezing out here."

"That just makes it more exciting." I shrugged my shoulders even though she was right. The creek that ran along the length of the campground was freezing on a normal day. It would be torturous on a night like tonight.

"I do not find hypothermia exciting." Frankie shook her head and held her hands out to the fire.

"Okay. You think of something then." I leaned back and rested my feet on the rocks that surrounded the fire pit.

"Truth or dare." Beck pressed a beer against my chest then moved around from behind us. "I'm sure we can dare

Frankie to jump in the creek, and you know she refuses to back down from a dare."

"Not true." Frankie shook her head. "I am not that competitive."

"Yes. You are." I laughed because she was one of the most competitive people I had ever met. Frankie usually ended up getting pissed almost any time we played any sort of board game and she didn't win. "I'm in."

"Where's Olly?" Josie looked behind us. "We need him to make this fun."

"I'm not fun?" I put my hand over my heart, completely offended.

"He's coming." Beck pulled up a chair right next to Josie and lifted her feet into his lap. "He was chopping some wood or some shit like that."

"What are y'all playing?" Allie asked from across the fire, and I avoided looking up at her.

"Truth or dare. Are you all in?" Josie asked, and I wished she hadn't. I had no interest in sitting here and playing a game with either of them.

"We'll play." Eli smiled down at Allie, and I leaned back in my chair to see who was at the next campsite.

"We're playing truth or dare!" I yelled out into the almost pitch-black. "Anyone want to join us?"

Josie smacked my arm, but I didn't care. We needed more people so I could be distracted. Otherwise, this wasn't going to be fun for anyone.

By the time the game started, Olly had made his way back, and Will Hollis and a few of his boys from his baseball team had made their way over. There were a few girls hanging around too, but I didn't recognize any of them.

"Okay." Beck rubbed his hands over Josie's feet. "What are the rules?"

I grabbed the bottle of whiskey I had gotten out of my tent and set it on the edge of the fire pit. "You get to pick whether you choose truth or dare, but then you have to complete the task. No passing. If you refuse, you have to take a shot of whiskey."

Some moaned while a few others laughed, but eventually everyone agreed.

"Okay. I'm first." Frankie grinned and sat up further in her chair with a blanket wrapped around her.

"Josie, truth or dare?"

"Ugh, seriously?" Josie looked over at Frankie. "Truth, because I'm too comfy."

"Who is the last person you creeped on social media?"

A couple people laughed, but Josie's face fell. "Frankie, I'm going to kill you."

"Answer or drink." Frankie grinned back at her best friend.

"Fine. It was Carson, and I'm not answering why."

"What?" I chuckled and stared at her.

Josie completely ignored my question and kept going. "Carson, truth or dare?"

"Dare," I answered easily. Doing whatever stupid dare she came up with would be so much easier than answering any of their nosy questions.

"I dare you to jump in the creek completely naked." She grinned as Frankie laughed next to her.

"Is this why you were stalking my social media? Were you trying to get a glimpse of a nude?" I stood from my chair and pulled my shirt over my head. If she thought I was going to back down from her dare, she was dead wrong.

"No!" she shrieked and her face turned red.

"You better get your girl, Beck." I looked over at my friend just as he rolled his eyes. Both of us knew without a doubt that Josie was absolutely and unconditionally in love with him. But God, she was fun to tease. "I think she might have a crush on me."

"You have a really big head, Carson." She crossed her arms, and I loved how embarrassed she looked as I kicked off my shoes.

"You're about to find out what else I have that's really big."

Allie snorted out a laugh, and for the first time in the last few minutes, I finally looked over the fire at her. She was watching me with her full attention. She had her knees pulled up against her chest, and everything inside of me begged me to cross the space that separated us and kiss the shit out of her.

Then I noticed Eli's arm around the back of her chair, and it was like a hard dose of reality.

I pulled my sweatpants down my hips and let them fall to my feet before I pulled them off and dropped them in my chair. "Do you want me to get completely naked right here, or should I spare all you guys so your girlfriends don't get all hot and bothered by your friend?"

"I say right here," one of the girls I didn't recognize called out and her friend laughed.

"All right. If you say so." I hooked my thumbs into the sides of my shorts and pushed them down.

There were a few shocked inhales, and I looked straight up at Allie because I couldn't help it. Her hand was over her mouth in shock, but she was looking directly at me. It didn't matter that Eli's arm was still wrapped around her. My girl was giggling along with everyone else, and her cheeks were red as she stared at me.

"Oh my God." Frankie died with laughter just as I turned back to her. "I cannot believe you just did that."

"That looks painful." Josie pointed at my cock, and I couldn't help laughing. I took off toward the creek, wincing as I stepped on rocks, and I could hear everyone's laughter behind me. Just as my feet hit the bone-chilling water, I heard Beck tell Josie to quit staring at me.

I laughed then took a deep breath.

"Putting your toes in doesn't count," Josie yelled from behind me. "You have to go in all the way."

I stepped in further, and for a second, I thought about walking my ass right back up there and taking a shot of whiskey. I didn't think this was worth it. Even if I did get to see all their faces when they saw my cock.

"I'm going." I waved her off, then sank down into the water until it ran over my chest. I could barely catch my breath as my body became pins and needles from the cold, but I quickly pushed beneath the water until I was completely covered.

As soon as I came up for breath, I jumped up out of the water and pushed myself back onto the bank. I was sure my cock was significantly less impressive now, but I didn't care. I was desperate to get back next to the fire and to get my dry clothes back on.

"Here." Beck threw me a towel as soon as I reached the edge of the campsite, and I rubbed it down my face before tucking it around my hips.

I quickly threw my shirt back over my head before tugging my sweats back up my legs sans underwear. I sat down in my chair and looked up at my friends.

"My turn?"

"Yep," Frankie answered and stared at me.

"What?" I chuckled as I slipped on my socks and shoes.

"Nothing." She shrugged her shoulders. "I'm just impressed, is all."

I chuckled and Beck shoved his sister's chair, almost making her fall. "That's my friend, asshole. You don't get to be impressed."

"No. She's right." Josie was still staring at me too. "I really expected you to have the smallest dick."

"I feel like I should be offended." I leaned back in my chair.

"It's your personality." Allie shrugged. "You know, cocky guy, small dick. Showy car, small dick."

"Okay, Allie." I pressed my elbows into my knees and looked across the fire at her. "Truth or dare?"

She stared at me, and I had a feeling that no matter what she picked she wouldn't do it. "Truth."

I let my gaze slide to Eli before it went back to her. I shouldn't have even called her name. I should just ask her something stupid and move on, but my heart raced in my chest, and I didn't hesitate with what I asked her next. "When was the last time that you were truly turned on? I mean really and truly, couldn't-think-about-anything-else turned on?"

A few people snickered, but I didn't look away from her. She didn't pull her gaze away from me either as she answered, but I knew her answer was a lie the moment it left her mouth.

"When Eli kissed me."

"Carson, truth or dare?"

"Truth."

"When was the last time you were really and truly turned on? And I mean to the point that you actually considered kissing the girl?"

"Oh shit." That came from Olly, but no one said anything to stop us.

"Just about any time I'm with you, but if you're looking for a specific moment, the night the cops walked in while I was going down on you."

Laughter rang out around us, but neither of us was deterred.

"Allie, truth or dare?"

"Truth." There was no hesitation in her eyes. She wasn't scared of what I had to say.

"Do you actually like Eli, or are you just pissed off at me?"

"This is the exact reason people think you have a small dick." She crossed her arms. "You assume that everything anyone does it about you when it isn't. I actually like Eli, for your information." She tucked a blonde curl behind her ear. "Carson, truth or dare?"

"This is about to get messy," Josie whispered to Beck, but I heard her. She was right. It probably was.

"Dare." I cocked my head to the side and looked at her.

"I dare you to stop being such an asshole and just tell us what the hell your problem is."

"My problem?" I rubbed at my jaw. "Currently my problem is you. You haven't barely spoken to me in days, you've been avoiding me like the plague at community service, and now..."

"Now what?" She was angry.

"Now I have to sit here and watch you with him." I pointed at Eli, and he had the nerve to fucking smirk at me.

"I haven't spoken to you because the last time we spoke, you made it very clear where we stood. I've been avoiding you because I don't want to deal with you, and you're going to have to continue to watch me with him because I like him. And it's the oddest thing, but he likes me too."

"Truth or dare?"

"I'm done playing this stupid game." She pushed out of her seat, and I knew that Eli was about to follow her.

"Truth or dare, Allie? It's not that hard."

She spun back around to face me, and I could see the anger in her eyes. "Fine. Dare." She held out her arms because she thought by ending the truths, she was going to end this argument between us.

"I dare you to kiss me."

"That's not happening." Eli had the balls to say that out loud to me, and it took everything inside me not to close the space between us and finish what we had started last weekend.

"The last time I checked, you weren't Allie's boyfriend, and you don't speak for her." I looked back to Allie, and she was staring at me. "Allie can either kiss me or she can drink." I lifted the bottle of liquor and shook it between us.

"You kissing me changes nothing." She shook her head.

"Then it won't hurt." I shrugged my shoulders and tried to act like I didn't care one way or another, even though I didn't know what would happen if she walked away from me now. "If you're so into Eli and kissing me won't change anything, then what are you so scared of?"

"I'm not scared." Her answer was immediate.

"Then come here."

Eli reached for her hand, but she pulled away before he could stop her. She didn't look back at him as she walked away. Her gaze was directly on me, and I knew that this was probably crossing a line I wasn't ready to cross.

I didn't know if I could handle the aftermath of my choices, but I did know that I couldn't handle her walking away with him. Everything about Allie was a double-edged sword.

She was heaven and hell. Everything I wanted and everything I was dying to run from.

She made her way toward me, and I looked up at her with a grin on my face as she stopped in front of me.

"Your choice." I held up the liquor to give her an easy way out if this wasn't what she wanted.

But she didn't hesitate. She leaned forward, her hand pressing into the armrest of my chair, and I noticed the trembling of her fingers. "You're such an asshole," she whispered the words just before her mouth came down against mine, and I froze.

I hadn't expected her to actually go through with it.

I just wanted to get under her skin. If I couldn't have her, I needed to get to her. It was a fucked-up logic, but it was the truth.

She gently kissed my mouth before pulling back slightly, but I couldn't let her walk away. I reached forward, gripping the back of her neck into my hand, and I pulled her mouth back down against mine.

It had been so long since I kissed anyone, and I didn't even really know why. But girls always expected too much when you kissed them. Sex was easy and detached, but kissing was something else.

It was personal and passionate, and in my experience, it tended to get everyone confused.

But I felt no confusion right now. I wanted Allie. I knew that fact with perfect clarity.

I pressed my lips to hers before tightening my hand on her neck and coxing her mouth open with the touch of my tongue. She let out the tiniest little whimper, and I took full advantage. I slipped my tongue across the seam of her lips before I slipped it inside. Her tongue met mine, and God, everything about her was so damn soft.

Her lips, her tongue, the skin of her neck beneath my fingers.

I demanded more from her, my tongue and lips and teeth kissing and nipping and lapping at her like she was everything I had ever wanted or needed.

But she didn't stop me.

She kissed me back just as hard. Every bit of anger she had just felt for me was poured into her kiss; every bit of her hate pressed into my lips.

I had thought about this moment for so damn long, but nothing that I had imagined had ever compared. Not even the moment I spent between her thighs compared to this.

Because as much as I gave Allie that day, right then, she was giving to me with just as much want. She kissed me like she was dying inside just like I was, and this kiss, this stupid damn moment in a game of truth or dare, felt like a lifeline.

Every part of my body felt alive as she kissed me. My cock was so hard that I knew everyone would notice when she walked away, but I didn't care. I wanted to kiss her forever.

"Carson," she whispered my name so softly that I doubted anyone around us heard, but it coursed through me like fuel.

My fingers threaded into her hair, and I pulled her down closer to me.

"Carson, stop." This time, her voice was firmer, and I ran my tongue over her bottom lip before I pulled back enough to look at her.

She was staring down at me, and there were tears in her eyes. She looked far more hurt than anything else, and it was like a hard dose of reality had washed over me.

"Allie," I said her name just as she pulled away and straightened to her full height. I didn't know what to say to her. I didn't know how to make her understand that I didn't know what the hell was going on.

I was so damn fucked up, and I couldn't figure out how not to be fucked up when it came to her.

I stood from my chair, but she immediately put her hand against my chest to stop me. She looked away from me quickly, then had a fake-ass smile on her face when she looked back.

"Ladies, he's not a half bad kisser either. It seems Mr. Unavailable here might be the full package."

There were a few chuckles around us, but I didn't give a shit about what any of these people thought. "Allie, let me talk to you." I placed my hands over hers where it rested on my chest, but she pulled it away and shook her head.

"Frankie, you take my next turn." She stepped back, and I reached out to steady her before she landed in the fire. "I'm going to go with Eli to get another drink."

She jerked her hand away from mine, and I watched her walk back around the campsite to where Eli waited for her. He looked pissed, but he still held his hand out for her and pulled her against his side as soon as she took it.

I wanted to scream at her and beg her not to leave with him, but I knew it wouldn't do any good.

God, we had just kissed, and she was already walking straight back to him.

I could do nothing but watch her.

CHAPTER 20
ALLIE

I stared up at the roof of the tent and prayed that I would fall asleep. I had been laying in this sleeping bag with Eli at my side for the last couple hours, and Eli had passed out almost as soon as his head touched the pillow.

Which meant I had the last couple hours to obsess over every single detail that happened tonight and the past few days before it. But more than anything, I had the past couple hours to completely be consumed by thoughts of kissing Carson.

I hadn't been ready for it. My heart wasn't prepared, and now it was all I could think about.

When he had dared me to kiss him, I was already so irritated with him. I didn't think he was actually going to do it. I thought he was just trying to prove a point, to throw me off my game. But there was no way that I was backing down to him.

I refused to allow him to think he won somehow.

But then when I kissed him, when he kissed me, it didn't

feel like some stupid dare that neither of us wanted to be a part of. Everything about it felt like it was exactly where I was meant to be. His hands were meant to be holding me in place, his fingers meant to be digging into my skin, and his lips were meant to be on mine.

It evoked everything inside of me that I had hoped Eli's kiss would have, but that kiss didn't stand a chance. But I already knew it wouldn't.

Carson was so damn hot and cold. He hated me then he wanted me, but through all of it, I knew exactly where I stood.

I had been in love with Carson Hale for as long as I could remember, and you don't just grow out of that.

He may have decided that he didn't want to be with me or be my friend or whatever the hell he thought he knew he wanted, but that didn't mean I wanted those things too.

But what I wanted had never mattered. Not when it came to him.

It couldn't matter now either.

Not when I was lying in a tent with someone else.

Someone else who hadn't even acted like he was angry with me for kissing Carson even though he had to be. I would be if I was him. But he wasn't an ass to me at all.

He stood there while I had tears in my eyes over another damn guy, and he simply smiled at me. And I felt like complete and total shit about it.

I felt like an even bigger piece of shit when he held me in the tent and kissed me gently. It felt wrong. Completely and utterly wrong, but I didn't stop him. I couldn't stop him because I was clinging to him and his kiss, and begging for it to mean more than it actually did.

But no matter how hard I kissed him or how much I

wanted it to be more, it wasn't. He wasn't Carson, and it didn't compare. Not when he pressed his hand against my breast through his sweatshirt or when the panic took over.

I wasn't ready for Eli to touch me that way. I wasn't sure that I would ever be, and I knew that had to piss him off. He had to listen to the things that I had let Carson do to my body, but I wouldn't let him touch me.

He hadn't made me feel bad about it, though. He simply kissed me again before he snuggled in against me and fell asleep. It was sweet and should have comforted me, but it was suffocating.

Everything about this entire trip was.

I gently lifted his arm off me and sat up. I needed to get out of this tent. I just needed something.

I slowly unzipped the tent, trying to make as little noise as possible, then slowly closed it back once I was on the other side. It was still pitch-black outside, the only light provided by the few dying fires at the center of each camp-site, but I couldn't bring myself to care.

I needed to breathe, to get fresh air, to not feel like I was trapped for just a few damn seconds.

I moved to the fire and set another small log on top of the orange embers. The heat warmed me but also reminded me of the chill beyond it, and I held my fingers out to absorb the warmth.

"Can't sleep?"

I jolted at the sound of Carson's voice and almost fell onto my ass. "Oh my God." I pressed my hand to my chest and looked up to find him in the same chair he was sitting in earlier. I hadn't even noticed him when I walked out. "You scared the crap out of me."

"I was sitting right here the entire time." He chuckled as he watched me.

I pushed my hair out of my face and stood. I looked back at my tent then back at him. "No. I can't sleep. You?"

"No." He shook his head. "I've got too much on my mind."

We were silent for a few minutes. It was awkward and tense, and I considered going straight back into my tent.

"Eli does not help you get to sleep?" Carson's jaw tensed as he said the words, and I knew that he was being an ass because it was his defense. This was his way of protecting himself from anything that he could possibly be feeling.

"Do you want to know if I slept with Eli? Is this your way of asking?"

He looked away from me to the tent, and he clenched his jaw so hard that I thought it might break.

"If you want to know, just ask." I crossed my arms and stared at him. The bottle of whiskey he pulled out earlier was by his side, and there was a lot missing. I didn't know if that was all due to him or if he had help, but he didn't look drunk.

"Fine." He brought his gaze back to me and there was a determination there. "Did you sleep with him?"

For a second, I thought about lying to him. I wanted him to be jealous of Eli. I wanted him to know what it felt like to hear about me with someone else, but I couldn't do it.

"Of course, I didn't sleep with him."

He nodded his head like he didn't really care either way, but I knew he did. He could say whatever he wanted, but it did matter to him.

"Why would it matter to you, though?" I laughed and looked up at the star-laden sky. "I think you just like fucking with me. Is that it? You just want to make sure I'm not happy with anyone?"

"You know that's not the truth."

"No. I don't." My laugh sounded insane. "I don't have the energy for this, Carson." I took a step back toward the tent and panic filled me. I didn't want to go in there, but I also didn't want to stay here.

I felt trapped between what I was and what I wanted to be, and I didn't know how to escape it.

I didn't know how to move out of this damn cycle that I felt like I couldn't evade.

"I just keep fucking this up." He looked so vulnerable as he said it, and I hated that my heart ached just looking at him.

"Fucking what up?"

"This." He waved back and forth between us. "I keep fucking up whatever the hell this is between us. I fucked it up when we were younger, and I keep fucking it up now."

My chest felt like it was caving in as he spoke. "When we were younger, you had to deal with something you should have never had to deal with, and you chose to push me away. I know that I hurt you then by going out with someone else, but I also know that you pushed me away because what happened with your parents scared you."

"I pushed you away." He leaned forward and pressed his elbows into his knees as he watched me. "Because I was too reliant on you. I pushed you away because I was so damn in love with you that I couldn't see anything else. You were my best friend then and I was such an idiot, but I knew that I couldn't rely on one person like that. Look what happened to my mom when she did."

I tried to catch my breath as I thought about what he just

said. He claimed that he had loved me back then, but I was the one who had been pining after him for years. I was the one who was absolutely devastated when he refused to talk to me anymore. I lost far more than my best friend that day.

"You know that you're not your parents, right? You are nothing like your dad or your mom."

He laughed and leaned back in his chair. "Of course, I am." He grinned as he rubbed at his jaw, and it was so damn fake. "These are the two people who raised me, and you think I'm nothing like them? Look at the way I treat women, Allie. That screams my dad, doesn't it?"

"Because you chose for it to." I held my ground because no matter how he pretended to act, I knew who he really was. "This is what you've chosen for yourself because you're scared to get hurt. Who knows." I shrugged my shoulders and tried to shield my heart. "Any one of those girls could have been the girl for you, but you never gave a single one of them a real chance."

"That's where you're wrong. You have a dreamer's heart, Allie, and it will eventually lead you to get married and have babies and maybe you'll be happy. But that kind of hopeless dreaming will get me nowhere."

"You don't know that." I felt so helpless in that moment thinking about Carson going through life and never finding someone to be happy with. Even if it most certainly was going to be someone who wasn't me.

"I do." He nodded toward my tent. "Any guy would be lucky to have you, Allie, but don't settle for some dirtbag. You deserve better." He stood from his chair and looked at me with such sad eyes before heading in the opposite direction to his tent.

"And are you better?" I questioned him. He didn't want me to be with Eli, but he didn't treat me like Eli did. He didn't act like someone who would deserve me if that was how he wanted to look at it.

"No." He chuckled and unzipped his tent. The sound was loud and rang out through the campsite, and I worried that it might wake everyone else up. "I'm far worse. I will never be good enough for you."

I knew that he was going to leave, to go inside his tent and end this conversation, and then tomorrow we would pretend like it never even happened, and I could feel the panic of that thought running through every part of me.

I didn't want to pretend like tonight hadn't happened. I didn't want to forget our kiss or this conversation or the fact that neither one of us could let each other go, even though we both desperately wanted to.

"Do you want to?" My voice was so soft I barely heard it.

"What?" He looked back at me.

"Do you want to be good enough for me? Has that thought ever crossed your mind?"

"Of course, it has." He ran his hand over his hair. "Of course, I wish things were different and that I was good enough for you, but that's not realistic. I can't wish for things that aren't ever going to happen. That's how you get disappointed."

I took a step closer to his tent, to him, and my heart raced. "Then let's just pretend."

"Allie, what are you talking about?"

"Just for right now." I didn't even know what I was saying, but I knew that I couldn't walk away from him and get back into that tent with Eli. Not tonight. "Let's just pretend like we're exactly what each other wants and that there is nothing that stands in our way."

"Then what?" He looked at me like I was going crazy, and maybe I was. "What will we do when tomorrow comes, and I'm no longer who you want and we both have to face reality?"

"We'll deal with it tomorrow." I got closer and closer to him and stopped when I was only about a foot away. This was his choice. If he wanted me to leave, then I would. If he didn't want me, he would have to be the one to stop this.

"You'll regret me." His gaze dropped to my mouth before coming back up.

"I haven't regretted you yet."

He stared at me for a few moments, and I thought I was going to die while I waited for him to make his decision about me, while I waited for him to decide if he would regret me.

"Take off his fucking sweatshirt." He looked so territorial as he said it, and I didn't hesitate. I pulled Eli's sweatshirt over my head and discarded it behind me. Then Carson reached out until my hand was in his, and he pulled me inside his tent.

My heart was hammering in my chest, and I couldn't think straight while he lowered the zipper of the tent door. He turned to me, and I didn't know what to do. I didn't know what to say or how to move forward.

But I didn't have to.

Carson closed the space between us and his hands cupped my face seconds before he brought his mouth down against mine. I let out my breath and he inhaled it. His teeth grazed my bottom lip before his tongue caressed the same spot, and I wrapped my fingers in his t-shirt.

I held on to him as his tongue met mine, and I refused to loosen my grip even when his own fingers tightened against me like he was scared I would disappear.

The kiss was everything it was during our game of truth or dare, but it was also everything it wasn't. It felt like pure longing and sin, but I knew that I wouldn't apologize for a second of it. I refused to apologize for a single moment with him.

His hands pushed into my hair, and he used them to tilt my head backward just the slightest bit as his thumbs ran up and down my throat. He kissed me harder as his body pushed into mine. I was already so turned on, and so was he.

He moved his mouth along my lips, then lower until they pressed into my jaw. I shivered, but it had nothing to do with how cool the night had become.

"Allie," he whispered my name against my neck, and it felt like a plea. Every syllable of my name falling from his lips tempting me to forget everything but him.

I pushed away from him, and there was a moment of hurt that flashed in his eyes before he watched me sink to the floor in front of him. I laid against his sleeping bag, and I prayed that he didn't change his mind and walk away.

But he dropped to his knees, pulling each of my legs on either side of his hips, then settled against me. He hovered over my body as he pushed some of my hair out of my face, then he was back to kissing me.

My body thrummed beneath him, and I didn't know where to touch him. I wanted to touch everything, to experience every piece of his body, but I was nervous.

My hands shook as I pressed them into his sides and clung to his t-shirt. I could feel his hard muscles beneath my fingers. They bunched and shifted as he used them to support his weight above me.

I wished he wouldn't. I just wanted him to fall into me and let me have all of him. I wanted to know what his weight felt like against me. I wanted to feel the heat of him against my skin.

I spread my legs further apart, making more room for him, and bent my knees at his sides. He was barely touching me anywhere except for my mouth and my face, but that wasn't enough for me. I felt like I was dying for him to touch me anywhere.

I lifted my ass off his sleeping bag until my hips met his. He groaned into my mouth, and it made me feel even hungrier. I wanted to hear that sound come from his mouth over and over again. I wanted to be the one to cause it, I wanted to be the one who drove him mad with my touch.

But I also knew that he had experienced this all before, and I tried not to let that thought eat at me. His experience didn't make what was happening between us now any less special.

It didn't make it any less real.

"Carson," I groaned his name when he did nothing but kiss me. It was wonderful, but it wasn't enough.

Not now.

"What, Allie? What do you want?" He pulled my bottom lip between his teeth before letting it go. He sat up onto his knees, and his gaze searched down my body as he ran his hand from my neck to the top of my shorts.

"I want you." It was the truth. I didn't know how else to answer him. I wanted whatever he was willing to give me.

His finger hooked underneath the waistband of my shorts, and he moved it back and forth gently as he watched it. "We don't have to do anything you don't want to do tonight."

I didn't answer him. Instead, I gently lifted my hips off the ground and let him pull my shorts down my legs. He lifted one foot after the other and pulled them off.

I sat up, and with shaking hands, I pulled my t-shirt over my head. I was face to face with him, and I was in nothing but my bra and panties. He still kneeled there fully dressed, but for some reason, I didn't feel self-conscious with him.

He dipped his head and pressed a kiss to the center of my chest, and I could feel his deep breath push in and out against my skin. He hesitated there, and I could feel him overthinking. I knew that he was so damn close to stopping what was happening between us, and it was the absolute last thing that I wanted.

The thought of him turning me away at that moment felt like it would destroy me.

So, I didn't give him the chance.

I pushed my fingers through his hair, and I tugged on the light strands until I forced him to look back up at me. I tried to ignore the doubt in his eyes, and I kissed him. I clung to him and tried to kiss every bit of that doubt out of his head.

I was so damn sure about him, and I needed him to be sure about me too. Even if it was just for this moment. I needed him to stop overthinking and worrying.

I pushed him off me and lifted onto my knees so I was level with him, and I tugged on the strands of his hair until I had enough leverage to run my mouth down the stubble of his jaw and down his neck.

"Allie." His chuckle was as soft as my name.

"Yeah?" I didn't lift my mouth from his skin. I let my teeth sink down into the soft skin of his neck gently before I lapped at the same spot with my tongue.

"What are you doing?" He moaned around the question, and his hands shook at my hips.

"Something I've thought about for a long time." I was finally honest with him. I ran my tongue along his earlobe before I whispered into his ear, "This is what I imagine any time I touch myself. Me touching you, you touching me, but you're never this hesitant." I pulled even harder on his hair, and he groaned loudly. "Just the other day I thought about what it would be like for you to be inside me. I thought about how good it would feel."

"Fuck." His hands tightened against my hips before he pushed me away from him. For a moment, I thought he was going to stop this, but he simply pushed me down against the sleeping bag before he jerked his t-shirt from his body.

It was like something had snapped inside him. Some thread of resistance he had been using against me. But it was gone now.

I could see it in his eyes that he was no longer willing to keep himself away from me.

He jerked my bra down and off my chest, and he was on me so quickly that I didn't have a chance to prepare.

He sucked my nipple into his mouth, and I was so unused to the sensation that I arched my back off the ground as I tried to take in the feeling. That only seemed to spur him on. He ran my nipple through his teeth before pressing his tongue flat against it, and his hand lifted to cup my other breast.

His hips were resting against mine, and I couldn't help the way I began to move my hips against him. I could feel how turned on he was. His sweatpants did nothing to hide that fact, and he felt so good against me.

I wrapped my legs around his hips, using his body as leverage to pull my own closer to him. His mouth worked me harder and faster the more I moved against him, and I felt like I was chasing something that I would never be able to find. Everything about this felt too good.

"Fuck, baby." He pulled my nipple into his mouth again before lifting and immediately jerking my panties down my thighs.

They were trapped just barely down my hips since my legs were still spread around him, but that didn't deter him in any way. He held the front of my panties in his hand, the material digging into my thighs, and forced them down as his tongue slid along the top of my pussy.

"Oh, God." I reached for his head and tried to force him to look at me, but he was too invested in what he was doing. "Carson, I want to touch you."

He looked at me then, and God, the look on his face was almost enough to make me fall completely apart. No matter what he said or what he tried to make me believe, I had no doubts that he wanted me. That one look alone proved that.

"I need to touch you first." He pressed the gentlest kiss just above my clit, and my hips jolted forward toward his mouth. "I need to be able to eat this pussy without anyone distracting us. I need to taste exactly what it's like for you to come on my face then kiss that taste from my lips."

"Oh, God." I looked up to the ceiling of the tent as my thighs shook.

"Look at me, Allie. I want to make sure you know exactly who it is that's giving this to you."

I looked back to him, and he held my gaze as his tongue

ran up the length of me then pressed roughly against my clit. He sucked it into his mouth, and it was almost too much. My hips rocked forward, but he forced them back down with his hand.

He pushed up onto his knees, and he forced my panties down my legs in quick, jerky motions. I expected him to fall right back into me, but he didn't. He fell to his back beside me, and he didn't say a word as he lifted me over him. I pushed against his chest for balance as I straddled his stomach, and I could feel my wetness against his skin.

He wrapped his hands behind my ass, and he pulled me forward until I was hovering just below his face. Panic took over, and I lifted my knee to move off of him, but he gripped my thighs in his hands to stop me.

"Ride my face, baby." He pulled me forward even harder until I was directly over his mouth, and he wasted no time before he dove into my flesh.

"Carson." I fell forward and my hands hit the ground as I tried to concentrate on what he was doing.

His hands cupped my ass, and he used them to force me to move. A job I took over as soon as I realized how good it felt, and I couldn't stop riding his face as he used his lips and tongue and teeth to drive me completely crazy.

He pressed his hand to my chest and pushed me backward. He stared up at me as he rubbed my nipple between his fingers. I rested my hands on his chest, giving him full access to mine, and I continued to ride him.

This position made me open even further to him, and I knew that I should have probably felt a bit embarrassed or self-conscious, but he didn't give me a single moment to even consider it.

I was already falling apart around him, and I couldn't focus on anything else.

"Carson," I cried out his name and tightened my thighs around his head. I didn't think I could handle this. The only orgasms I had ever experienced was the one he had given me and the ones I had given myself, but this felt so much bigger than both of those.

He wrapped his hands around my legs, his fingers digging into the sensitive skin of my inner thighs, and he forced my legs back apart.

It was too much.

Everything about it was perfect and too much. Mesmerizing and torturous.

I pressed my hand against my mouth as I cried out, but I didn't think it did much to hide the sound. We were surrounded by so many other people, one person who I was currently supposed to be asleep beside, but Carson didn't care.

He continued his assault until I could no longer hold myself upright, and only then did he kiss my inner thigh and roll me over onto my back.

I laid there lifeless for a moment as he continued kissing up and down my stomach, but even as satisfied as I was at that moment, I knew that I had to touch him, to taste him, to make him feel exactly like he had just made me.

But more than anything, I wanted Carson to be inside me. I wanted to know what it felt like for him to be that person. It was always him, and I couldn't imagine giving my virginity to anyone else.

I sat up, pushing him down as I went, and I moved down his body until my hand rested on his lower stomach. My fingers shook as I moved them even lower. Carson gripped my wrist in his before I could go beneath his pants, and I looked up at him.

"Kiss me," he demanded, and I didn't argue. I leaned forward and kissed him as fiercely as he had kissed me only moments before. I could taste myself on his lips, and I was shocked to find out how much that turned me on.

Carson's mouth was covered in everything he had done to me, and the combination of me and him was intoxicating.

He buried his hand in between my thighs as I kissed him, and I jumped at the shock of how sensitive but how turned on I was.

"I want to taste you," I whispered and looked up at him.

"You don't have to." He shook his head, but I was already moving down his body.

"I know, but I want to." My trembling fingers tugged at the top of his waistband, and he lifted enough that they easily slipped down past his hard cock. He was much bigger than I would have imagined, and seeing it this up close and personal was intimidating.

I ran my fingers over him, and I was shocked by how soft his skin was. He hissed as my skin met his, and I was in love with the sound. My touch was hesitant as I explored him, and I avoided looking up at Carson.

"Have you ever..." His voice trailed off, but I knew what he was asking.

"No." I shook my head quickly. "I've never done anything if it wasn't with you."

He groaned deep and loud, then he made a fist around mine. "Like this." He stroked my hand up and down his cock, and I got a feel for how hard he liked it. "You won't hurt me." He continued to work my hand up and down him. "Anything you do feels amazing."

He dropped his hand from mine, and I continued to pump my hand up and down him like he showed me. His head fell backward, and he swore, and I could see a bead of moisture leak from the tip of him. I leaned forward following the path of my hand, and I ran my tongue directly over the tip and tasted him.

"Fucking hell." His hips surged forward, and he hit my tongue again before sliding into my mouth.

This time I didn't stop. I lowered my mouth around him, and I took as much of him into my mouth as I could manage as my hand continued to move at the base of him. His fingers tangled in my hair, but he didn't force my head one way or another. He simply held on to me as I fucked him with my mouth, and I started moving faster and faster against him as I got the hang of it.

"Allie, baby." His fingers tightened in my hair as he groaned. "I'm going to come in your mouth if you don't stop."

I didn't stop. I just worked him faster with my hand and my mouth, and I looked up at him to see him staring down at me. He was watching my every movement, and I felt so powerful. His body was trembling beneath my hands because of the things I was doing to it.

He was right on the edge, and I was the one who put him there.

He sat up, reaching his hands under my armpits, and he lifted me. My mouth left his cock, and my hands pressed into his shoulders as he forced me up and over his lap. I settled against him, and I could feel the hard length of him beneath me.

I shifted, forcing myself to slide against him, and his

deep groan rang out through the tent. He buried his hand in the back of my hair until he brought my mouth to his.

I didn't stop moving against him as he kissed me. He felt too good, and I wasn't willing to let this moment stop.

"Allie," he murmured my name, but I still didn't stop.

"Yeah?" I gripped his shoulders and ground down harder. His cock was perfectly pressed against me, and it hit my clit with every movement I made.

"We don't have to do this. We don't need to go any further." His hand caressed my face and pushed a stray hair back as he searched my eyes.

"I want to." I swallowed and steeled my spine for what I was going to say next. "I want you to be my first. I want you to give me more than you've ever given any of them."

"Fuck," Carson cursed as his lips hit mine and kissed me like he wasn't sure if I was really there. His kiss was rough and hard and bruising, but it was also exactly what I needed.

Carson leaned to the side and fumbled in his bag before he pulled out a condom. I watched as he ripped the wrapper open with his teeth then lifted me to my knees before sliding the condom over his cock.

He looked up at me once the condom was fully in place, and I knew that he was questioning this decision. He was worried that I was making the wrong decision, but he was wrong. I had thought about this moment for as long as I could remember, and I couldn't imagine anyone else being my first.

Even if Carson and I walked away from this with nothing else, I would still have this. I would know that I gave my virginity to a boy who cared about me whether he wanted to admit it or not.

I was giving it to a boy who was so damn broken, but someone who had also been my best friend.

I pushed further onto my knees before he could even consider stopping me, and I reached between us to line him up with me. I had no idea what I was doing, but I knew that I wanted this.

He wrapped his fingers over mine with one hand and used the other to push my moisture around. "You are so fucking wet," he whispered before sliding a finger inside me.

"Carson." I pressed my face into his neck and tried to breathe through the pleasure he was giving me.

"I got you, baby." He pulled his finger out and slid that moisture all around me until he was circling my clit.

I whimpered just as he pressed the head of him against me. He didn't stop rubbing my clit as he slid me slowly down him. I tried to focus on what he was doing, but it was so hard. The pleasure he gave me was so overwhelming.

He let go of his cock and brought his hand out and onto my ass, then he guided me ever so slowly to lower myself down onto him. There was a slice of pain as he began to fill me, but he held me still as I winced and brought my pleasure back to the forefront of my mind.

He repeated that process over and over until I was completely settled against him. I felt so damn full with him inside me and so damn overwhelmed, but Carson didn't give me time to overthink. He continued to rub circles on my clit and his tongue chased the same pattern against my neck.

I began to move against him, and I felt like I was trying to outrace my thundering heart. Carson let me have control. I rode him gently at first until the edge of pain all but disappeared, then I moved faster and faster, and when I was finally used to the feeling, he lifted me off him and climbed to his knees.

He moved me to my knees, turning me away from him before sliding inside me again. My back pressed against his chest as he began to move, and I cried out at the first slide in and out of me. It felt so different in this position, so overwhelming and delicious, and there was something about him being in complete control as he thrust up into me that felt intoxicating all on its own.

He slid his hand back down to my clit while the other held me firmly against his chest, and he set a rhythm that made my head spin. I couldn't keep up with the feel of his hands, of him inside me, of the way he nipped at my neck.

"I'm…" I tried to catch my breath, but it was all too much. "I'm going to come, Carson."

He slid his hand to my neck and tilted my head until I was looking back at him. He didn't slow his onslaught of my pussy as he kissed me. My back was slick with sweat that glided between us, but I didn't care. I kissed him with as much passion as he was giving me, and I was chasing his tongue as I chased the feeling over the edge.

Carson's fingers squeezed my neck harshly as he thrust up into me, and I cried out as my orgasm coursed through every part of me. I couldn't hold myself upright, but I didn't have to. Carson held me against him as he moved beneath me, and it was only moments later when he groaned against my back and fell over the edge himself.

We sat exactly where we were for a few moments, the only sound around us was both of us trying to catch our breaths, but Carson lifted me off him. I winced as he slid out of me and suddenly felt so self-conscious as I moved beside him.

I grabbed my t-shirt and quickly threw it over my head as I searched the small space for my shorts. Carson pulled the condom from him and tied it in a knot before laying it to the side, and I could feel my heart racing as he looked back at me.

I didn't know what to do or what to say now. I hadn't really thought this through when I walked into this tent, but the reality of what we had just done was hitting me now. I didn't regret a second of it, of course I didn't, but I was still scared of the consequences.

The consequences that would come from him.

Because I knew that what we just did would affect him, and I didn't know how he would react. I lifted his t-shirt off the ground and searched for my shorts. My hands started to shake when I couldn't find them. I needed to get out of this tent, out of his space. I didn't know where I was going to go as there was no way in hell I would go back to my tent with Eli still in it, but I knew I needed to leave here.

"What are you doing?" Carson's gruff voice sent chills down my spine.

"Looking for my clothes." I still didn't see them anywhere.

"Are you in a rush to leave?" He chuckled, and I swear the sound was like a hammer in my chest.

"I don't want to overstay my welcome." I turned to him and smiled. I needed to play this off like I wasn't falling apart inside. The last thing I needed was for him to know what I was feeling. If he had a glimpse of what was going on inside me, he would have already forced me out the door.

"Come here." He slid his hand against mine and tugged me toward him.

"What?" My chest hit his, and he searched my face. I

hoped that I had become good enough at hiding my feelings for him over the years that I was still capable of keeping them hidden now.

"Don't leave." He pushed my hair out of my face then pulled his sleeping bag open. He was still completely naked, and he made no moves to change that. He lifted his legs and slid into his sleeping bag, then held it open for me.

"I don't know." I looked from him to the spot he was making for me, and I absolutely knew what I wanted to do.

"Come on." He laid his head against his pillow and looked up at me. "We'll deal with everything tomorrow, but tonight is tonight. We agreed not to worry about all of this tonight, and I can already see every possible scenario running through your mind."

He was right, of course. That was exactly what we had agreed to, but it felt so reckless now. I had just given him so much of me, and I was still willing to give him everything. Climbing into his sleeping bag and pretending like those feelings wouldn't matter tomorrow felt like the most reckless decision I was going to make all night.

But I still climbed into the sleeping bag and let him hold me against him. I snuggled into his chest as he wrapped his arms around me, and I felt so damn safe there. I felt untouchable even though I knew I was far from it.

He pressed a kiss to the top of my head as he tightened his arms around me, and I let myself fall further and further into him.

Our legs were laced through one another, and our stomachs moved in sync as we breathed. This was the last place that I had expected to end up tonight, the last place I thought I wanted to be, but I didn't want to be anywhere else.

Carson had been my enemy for so long, but he had never really been that to me at all. He was the boy who I had once loved, and the boy who had broken my heart almost every day since then.

He was the boy who I had never fallen out of love with, and now I was going to have to figure out how to guard my heart from him once again. I was in love with him, but that didn't matter.

Carson Hale didn't love me, but I would face that fact tomorrow.

CHAPTER 21

CARSON

The sound of people outside my tent pulled me from my sleep. The sun was already so damn bright, but I felt like I barely had any sleep. Allie was lying against my chest with her arm wrapped around my side.

My arm beneath her was half asleep, but I never wanted her to move. I wished that the people talking would go away and not break this bubble we had around us.

Because last night had been perfect. It had been more than perfect. It had been everything.

And even though she started to freak afterward, I knew that she had felt it too.

"It's freezing out here," Josie's voice carried into the tent, and Allie stirred beside me.

Neither of us had really thought this morning through. I didn't care what any of these people thought. When she walked out of my tent this morning, I was perfectly fine with them knowing exactly where she had been.

But I wasn't sure if she was.

"Good morning," I whispered against the side of her

head, and she groaned as she blinked her eyes open and stretched. She was still wearing nothing but her t-shirt, and I was dying to touch her again.

I didn't care that there were people right outside the thin walls of the tent. Last night did nothing but stoke my want for her.

I cupped her ass in my hand and pulled her tighter against me.

"Good morning." She smiled and leaned into my touch.

"Is everyone else already awake?" She leaned back to look, but all you could see were shadows.

"I've heard a few of them." I tightened my hands around her because I wasn't ready for this to end. I wasn't ready to share her with the rest of the world.

"I should probably get up." She moved to sit up, but I refused to let her. I refused to just let her walk out of here after the night we had last night. Because I knew that once we walked out of this tent, this moment would be gone.

Everything would be different.

Reality would set in.

"Wait." I pressed my lips against her neck, then caressed the skin gently as I moved to her mouth. "I'm not ready to give you up yet."

"You don't have to." Her gaze met mine, and my chest tightened. She didn't know what she was saying. Everything that happened between us last night, everything that had happened over the last several weeks, it would all be ruined once she left this tent.

Because as much as I hated Eli, I knew that I was no better than him. I had jumped on that damn bet so quickly, and I did it trying to act like I was some knight in shining armor. I wasn't.

I was just desperate to have an excuse to get close to the girl I had been in love with so long that it was pathetic.

She was too good for me, and I knew. But I was far too selfish to stay away from her. Even if that meant that I only got these moments with her. Even if that meant that she would hate me after she found out the truth.

At least the truth that everyone else knew. My truth was different. My truth was that this was never about that damn bet. Yes, I wanted to protect her and keep her away from Eli, but more than anything, I just wanted her to myself.

"Just give me a few more minutes," I whispered against her lips. "I just need a few more."

She grinned against my mouth, and I knew she thought that I meant I needed a few more minutes with her because I wanted her body. I did, but that wasn't what I needed. I just needed to hold on to her for a few more minutes where nothing else could touch us. Where she was mine.

I slid my hand down her stomach, and she whimpered against my mouth. I cupped her pussy in my hand before sliding my finger inside gently. She was already wet, but I knew she was probably sore from the night before.

Ever so slowly, I moved my middle finger against her clit as I watched her face. She was looking at me like I was capable of giving her everything she ever wanted, but I wasn't. I was just capable of giving her this.

Everything else would crumble beneath my touch.

Everything else she wanted felt too far out of my reach.

"Has anyone seen Allie?" I heard Eli's voice, but I didn't care. I wasn't finished with Allie, and I wasn't letting her walk out of this damn tent until she rode this orgasm out.

If it was the only thing I could give her, then I would make sure that she remembered it. I wanted to be sure she always thought of me any time her own hand touched her body.

I wanted her to want me as desperately as I wanted her.

"Shhh," I whispered in her ear, and she moaned against my hand.

She made no move to care that Eli was looking for her or the fact that we could hear everyone else talking about her now as well.

"I thought she was asleep in there with you," Frankie said with an edge of worry in her voice.

"She was, but I woke up and she was gone."

"You didn't hear her leave your tent?" Beck barked at him, and I continued rubbing small circles against Allie's clit as I began pumping my finger into her.

She was so damn close. Her body was so tight against me, and she felt like she was going to snap and shatter at any moment.

"Carson," she whispered my name before looking to the side of the tent, but I refused to allow them to ruin this for us.

"No." I shook my head and guided her face back to mine. "Just me and you." I lifted her knee and spread her open further.

She pressed the blanket to her mouth to block her cries, but I was desperate for them. I wanted to be surrounded by her cries of pleasure, and I didn't give two fucks who heard them. I didn't care if Eli heard every moment of me giving her everything that she wanted.

I pulled the blanket away, and my lips hit hers. I kissed her as I pumped my finger in and out of her. She kissed me back like she was dying for my mouth. She kissed me like she was scared that this was all about to end, and I didn't blame her.

It was the only thing I could think about too.

I wanted Allie. Everything else be damned.

My own stupid, reckless choices be damned.

I wanted her regardless of every fear that I had.

But I didn't know how far this went for her. Last night we had agreed not to think beyond one night, but I think we both knew that was impossible.

I didn't need last night to overthink about her.

Every thought I had felt like a war with myself. I was determined to have her but destined to hurt her, and I couldn't fathom which was worse. Having a life without Allie in it, or having a life that was once filled with her that I ruined.

"Where the hell can she be? I knew one of us was going to get eaten by a bear!" Josie's voice rang out through the entire campground, and if I wasn't so close, I would have died laughing.

Allie looked worried even though her breathing was rushed, and her pussy was so damn wet around my hand. I pushed my fingers through her hair and forced her to look up at me.

"Look at me," I groaned and moved harder against her. "Nothing else matters. Me and you. Let go, baby."

She bit down on her bottom lip and arched her chest. She searched my eyes, and I knew that she was right there. I kissed her again just as her body tightened beneath my hands, and she moaned into my mouth as her hands clung to my chest.

"Oh, God." She kissed me so hard that I could think of nothing else. I pushed my finger inside her over and over until she slowly came down, and the urge to tell her that I loved her overwhelmed me.

"Carson!" Olly banged against my tent wall, and Allie jumped against me. "Get up, man."

"I need to go out there." Allie pushed on my shoulders to shove me away from her, and I let her.

"Here." I pressed my t-shirt against her and cleaned her up as she sat up. She looked embarrassed, but I couldn't bring myself to care after everything we had just done.

She let me clean her up, then she scrambled to grab her clothes and pull her shorts up her legs. I tugged my sweats on and handed her the bra, and she quickly slid it on before pushing her hair back out of her face. There was so much panic starting to show on her gorgeous face, and I absolutely hated it.

I didn't want her to be embarrassed or ashamed of being here with me, but I knew why she was. She was meant to be in her tent with Eli last night, but she was here with me instead.

She squatted down and pulled the zipper open to my tent door, but I stopped her as soon as she stood.

There was nothing I could say to make anything easier or better for her. There was nothing that I could whisper to her that would make her understand exactly what I was feeling so instead, I kissed her one last time, and I prayed that she could feel everything that was left unsaid between us.

I let her go, and she looked up at me just as we heard everyone starting to panic outside the tent.

"Calm down," I called out and searched her eyes one more time before I pushed out of the tent. I blinked as the sun blinded me and pulled a t-shirt over my head.

"We can't calm down." Frankie looked like she was going to kill me at the suggestion. "We can't find Allie."

It was at that exact moment that Allie climbed out of my tent, and it felt like I was watching a train wreck.

Frankie's mouth went slack as she watched her friend, and Olly immediately started laughing.

"What's so funny?" Josie turned from where she was standing with Eli to look in our direction, and I was pretty sure I heard her gasp.

But it wasn't until Eli turned and looked at Allie that I felt my stomach tense with anticipation. He looked back and forth between Allie and me, and he was pissed. Not that I blamed him. I would have been pissed too, but this wasn't about him.

It never had been.

He didn't care about Allie, but I did.

"Were you in his tent?" Eli pointed toward where we clearly just came from, and it took everything inside me not to smart off. I wanted to tell him that of course she came from my tent because Allie was mine, but I knew that wouldn't make anything easier on her.

And she already looked like she was regretting her decisions.

"Eli, can we talk?" She stepped toward him, and I wanted to pull her back to me. I didn't want her anywhere near him.

He ran his fingers through his hair as he looked back and forth between us again. "Yeah." He laughed without an ounce of humor.

She didn't look back at me as she made her way toward him, and I hated it. I hated every damn second of it.

I couldn't stop the feeling of dread with every step she

took. I didn't want her to forget what had happened between us. I didn't want her to forget how it felt.

"Allie," I called out her name just as she stepped beside him, but I had no idea what to say.

She looked back at me for only a second before turning back to Eli.

"It looks like you won, huh, Hale?" Eli held out his arms before turning back to Allie, and pure fucking dread filled me.

"Won what?" Allie asked, looking back and forth between me and Eli.

"Nothing," I answered at the same time as Eli said, "The bet."

"Shut the fuck up, Eli." I moved toward him, but Olly put a hand on my chest.

"What bet?" Allie demanded with her hands balled in fists at her sides.

"I told you." I shook my head and looked at her. "I told all three of you that Eli was only in this for a bet." I hated saying those words out loud because I knew they would hurt her. Even if she didn't care about Eli, that fact would hurt her, and I hated it.

"Right." Eli laughed again. "But I guess you left out the part where you took part in that bet too, huh? You did bag her just in time, though. Lucas is planning to tally up the score tonight."

I was going to kill him.

Allie stared up at me and I could see tears in her angry eyes. "This was all about a bet."

"Allie," I called her name, but she shook her head.

"You are a piece of shit, Carson."

"This had nothing to do with a stupid bet, Allie. You fucking know that."

"I don't know anything," she screamed at me. "You're telling me you didn't enter into this bet with them?"

I felt like I was drowning because I couldn't lie to her. I couldn't look her in the face and tell her what she wanted to hear. "I only did it to keep him away from you."

"What a joke." She turned to walk away from the both of us, but I quickly caught up to her and grabbed her hand in mine.

She jerked it from my grip and spun around on me. "Do not touch me again, Carson. You got what you wanted. Leave me alone."

I could feel everyone watching us, but I didn't give a shit about any of them.

"Allie, please," I begged her, and the look that crossed her face gutted me.

"You were right, Carson." She shook her head as a tear fell down her cheek. "You are exactly like your father."

I tried to catch my breath as her words hit me. She was angry and hurt, but God, she was right. I wasn't any better than him, and I would never deserve a girl like Allie.

She deserved so much better.

And I would never be the guy to give her that.

Keep reading for a sneak peek of...

The
DECEIT
of a
DEVIL

CHAPTER 1
ALLIE

I walked through the gate and grimaced when I saw Mr. Sneed waiting on me.

I was late, and I was one hundred percent sure that he noticed. Not only was I late, but I also hadn't shown up for the last week and a half. According to my mother, he wasn't very happy about it, but at this point, I really didn't have the energy to care.

"It's nice to see you show up." Mr. Sneed crossed his arms where he leaned against the porch. It looked like Carson had done quite a bit of work while I wasn't here.

I shrugged and looked around before tucking my hair behind my ear. "I wasn't feeling very good."

"Your friend said it was his fault." He nodded over his shoulder, and I knew that he was referring to Carson. He was here, and he was the absolute last person I wanted to see. "He's been working double to make up for you not being here."

"What a hero," I answered sarcastically, shocking Mr. Sneed.

"Are you two fighting?" He cocked his head to the side.

"Nope." I looked around the yard and tried to find something to do that would keep me as far away from Carson as possible. "We're exactly how we've always been."

It wasn't a complete lie. Everything I thought I had become with Carson was nothing but a lie. It was nothing but a damn game.

What we were was exactly what he had made us.

Enemies.

We had been that for a long time, but I had always hoped... I had wished things were different.

All that naivety was gone now.

I knew that we would never be anything more than exactly what we were, and I shouldn't have been angry about it.

But I was.

I was beyond angry and hurt, and I hated that I had given him the opportunity to make me either of those things. Carson was only able to hurt me because I cared about him when I shouldn't have. I cared about him, and I was even stupid enough to think that I might have loved him.

That seemed like nothing but a joke now.

"Okay." Mr. Sneed stood and his keys jangled in his hand. "I'm going to leave you two to it then. Carson's working on scraping off the peeling paint in the dining room now. He'll show you what he's been up to."

Awesome.

I nodded my head and climbed the old stairs that led into the house. I could do this. I kept telling myself that over and over. I was strong enough to face him. I was more than capable of pretending like I was completely and utterly unaffected by him.

Even though I had barely left my bed over the past week.

I could hear him working as soon as I stepped through the door, and I closed my eyes and took a deep breath as I pushed the door closed behind me. Josie and Frankie had offered to take over my community service duties for the rest of my time with Carson, but it didn't work that way.

Not only would Mr. Sneed not allow it, but there was no way I would let them do all this work for something I did.

Because at the end of the day, I was the one who agreed to sneak into this property with Carson, and I was the one who had let him touch me so inappropriately in this house. I was the one who had trusted him even though he had proven to me time and again that he wasn't worthy of it.

He was squatted down and running a paint scraper over the wall as I walked in. He was dripping with sweat, and he was wearing nothing but a pair of old jeans and tennis shoes. His discarded shirt was laying on the dirty floor with his bottle of water, and I wished he would put it back on.

Jerk or not, he was still one of the most attractive guys I had ever seen.

"Where do I need to start?"

He jumped, the sound of my voice clearly scaring him, and I found myself grinning when he almost landed on his ass.

"Allie," he said my name like it meant something to him, like I meant something to him, but I knew that was just another one of his games. Carson was the master of fucking with my head, and that was what he did every single time he called me and text me and showed up at my house since the moment I left our camping trip.

He fucked with my head.

But I no longer trusted anything about him or anything he said or did.

"It looks like you've already finished the living room." I looked over my shoulder to avoid looking at him and his sad eyes. "I can start in the hallway."

He stepped toward me and reached out his hand before thinking better of it and dropping it to his side. "Can we talk?"

"About what?" I sounded so disinterested, and I knew that he heard it too.

"About us."

I laughed and tucked my hands in my back pockets. "There is no us, Carson. Do you have an extra paint scraper, or do I need to go get one from Mr. Sneed?"

He clenched his jaw and watched me, and I knew that he wanted to argue. It wasn't an argument that he would win. "I have an extra."

He bent down to scoop up the tool, then handed it out to me. I grabbed it, careful not to touch him, but he refused to let go.

"Drop it, Carson," I growled at him.

"I don't want to." I knew he wasn't talking about the tool, but I didn't care what he wanted. I used to care, I cared more than anything, but not anymore.

"It doesn't matter what you want." I shrugged and jerked the tool from his hand. "Or is this about more than me and you?" I looked around the room dramatically. "If you need me to do something for you to win a bet, please let me know so we don't have to draw this out."

"You know this isn't about any stupid bet."

"I don't know anything." I could feel my heartbeat rising,

and I was so damn angry with him. "And I cannot trust a word you say. Should I call Eli?"

"Don't." He shook his head, and there was so much anger hidden in his eyes. But he had no right to be angry. He didn't have the right to feel anything.

"Don't what?" I laughed and walked away from him. "I can do whatever I want, Carson. It's not up to you."

"Not with him."

I spun around to find him following me, and I waved my hand in his direction, pointing the paint scraper right at him. "You don't get a say in whether or not I do anything with him. If I wanted to, I would leave here right now and go fuck him."

"I will kill him."

"For what?" I held my hands out as I tried to grasp exactly what the heck was going through his head. "Doing the exact same thing you did? You took my virginity. You won the bet. What else could you possibly want?"

"I know that I fucked up." He ran his hand over his sweaty hair. "But I am not him. I did what I did to keep him away from you. I tried to tell you what they had planned but you didn't listen. I knew the only way to get you to stay away from him was to get you to spend time with me. I didn't think..."

"You didn't think." I held on to the tool so tightly that my knuckles turned white. I wasn't ready to face him. I wasn't ready to have this conversation about what I thought we were and what we actually became. "You aren't some hero, Carson. You hurt me because you wanted to. You hurt me because you have some fucked-up grudge against me because of your own parents."

"Don't go there, Allie."

"I can go wherever I want." I raised my voice but tried to remind myself to calm down. He didn't deserve to see how affected I was by him. He and Eli and everyone else at the campground had already gotten to see how affected I was when I found out the truth. "I have tiptoed over talking about our past with you for so long that I'm freaking sick of it. I wasn't the one who cheated on your mom, and I wasn't the one who tried to kill herself, Carson."

He winced, and I knew I should have stopped. But this was a conversation we should have had a long time ago.

"I was your friend and you pushed me away because you needed someone to put the blame on for how hurt you were. I used to be fine with taking that from you, but I'm not anymore." I straightened my spine. "Grow the hell up, Carson."

I turned my back on him again when he didn't reply and headed to the hallway, even though being in this house with him was the absolute last place I wanted to be.

But I stopped dead in my tracks at the next sound of his voice.

"If he touches you, I'll kill him."

"What?" I looked over my shoulder, and he was staring at me like he actually meant what he was saying.

"Eli. If he lays a single finger on you, I will kill him."

Then he walked back the way he came, and I focused on my work.

CHAPTER 2
CARSON

I was so damn ready for this day to be over.

I couldn't focus on what our teacher was talking about. I hadn't heard a single word from her in over an hour. Instead, I tapped my pencil against my notebook and tried not to think about Allie.

But that was impossible.

Every single thought I had these days was about her. About how badly I had fucked things up with her. I obsessed over how mad she was, over how I could possibly get her to forgive me, and how I couldn't sleep because she wouldn't talk to me.

The final bell rang, and I snatched my shit up from my desk and was out of the room before anyone else. I felt like I was suffocating in there.

I was suffocating everywhere except when I was with her, and even then, it was torturous. Because she refused to even speak to me.

Not since that first day she came back to our community

service, and I was pretty sure I was running out of those silent days with her. Mr. Sneed hadn't yet told us when he was going to let us off the hook for our community service, but the house was already looking like a different place altogether.

He told us yesterday that he would have paint ready for us to paint over the signature wall when we got there tomorrow, and I was dreading it. She had done nothing but nodded her head, then left without a single word to me.

Mr. Sneed had given me a look of sympathy, and I knew that I was really fucked then.

I pushed through the locker room, and it was still silent. I shoved my shit into my locker before pulling out my practice gear. Being at baseball practice was the last place I wanted to be, but I knew that it would do me good.

It would take away some of that pent-up anger I couldn't seem to get under control. Even smoking and drinking hadn't helped, and trust me, I had tried. Olly was still a little pissed off after he had to take care of my drunk ass last weekend.

But as soon as I woke up the next morning, I had felt exactly the same. Worse almost.

And part of me had thought about just taking any girl up on their offer and trying my hardest to fuck the thoughts of Allie away, but I couldn't. Just thinking about it made me sick.

I couldn't do it after everything that had happened between us. Even if she hated me now. I didn't know how I could possibly touch another girl again, and that fucked with my head more than anything.

I was so damn wrapped up in her that nothing that used to matter to me mattered anymore.

I had been so worried about not getting too dependent on her and her on me that I didn't realize I was falling for her all along while simultaneously pushing her away. Now I was the one who needed her, and she didn't need or want a single thing from me.

The guys started filtering into the locker room, and I took a deep breath as I tried to prepare myself to face them. Eli and Lucas smirked and dug at me any chance they could. They knew that I had fucked up and that their stupid little fucking plan had been my downfall all along.

Beck and Olly had wanted to kill Eli after he told Allie the truth about what I had done, but it was pointless. He was telling her the damn truth while I was hiding it from her. I had painted him as the villain, but he wasn't any more villainous than I was.

Allie had been my best friend once, and I had still chosen to go through with my fucked-up plan. It didn't matter that I had started it as a way to keep them away from her; I knew what I was doing. I was desperate to be around her, to have an excuse to have her in my life again, and I took advantage of the situation.

And when things changed, when they had become more, I should have been honest with her, but I wasn't. And I took things too far.

I took things from her that I didn't deserve. She gave those things to me, and I knew she regretted that decision now.

And that was what hurt the most out of all of this. Allie had given me her body, her trust, she had given me things that she hadn't ever given to anyone else, and I ruined every bit of it.

And even though I wanted to kill both Eli and Lucas, I

knew that it was my fault. I could blame them all I wanted but everything that happened between Allie and me was my fault. I knew that fact as well as she did.

Because Allie hadn't even looked at Eli after she found out. His betrayal hadn't bothered her at all. It was me and my lies that had broken her. It was me and my lies that had fucked everything up.

I would always fuck everything up when it came to her. That was who I was. Eli may not have been good enough for her, but neither was I.

"What are you doing?" Beck tossed his bag down on the bench before opening his own locker and pulling out his gear.

"Just getting ready for practice." I pulled on my cleats and tried to focus on tying the laces. I tried to focus on anything other than the repetitive what-ifs that ran through my head. "Where's Olly?"

"I don't know." Beck threw his button-down into the locker before pulling an old t-shirt over his head. "He's been a bit distant lately. I think something might be going on with him."

I winced because, who the hell didn't have something going on at this point? But also, because I knew that the only thing Olly wanted to have going on was something with Frankie, and that was never going to happen. "Hopefully he's just getting laid or something."

"I was hoping that you'd be the one getting laid." Beck pulled his cleats out of his locker and sat down beside me. "You've been in a bad fucking mood."

"Yeah. I'm aware." I looked over at my best friend and part of me just wanted to unload everything on him, but this wasn't the time or the place. And I wasn't sure if I was willing to let Beck or Olly in on all the shit I had going on in my head. "But I don't really think getting laid is the answer right now."

"Since when?" Beck looked at me, really looked at me, and I knew that he was trying to figure out what was going through my head. Beck always knew when something was off with me. "You know if you fuck things up further with Allie that the girls are going to kill you, right?"

"To be honest, I really don't care what the girls think." I shrugged my shoulders because it was the truth. I loved Frankie and Josie, but their opinions didn't really matter when it came to Allie. I knew that they only wanted what was best for her, but I also knew that neither one of them believed that was me. "But I don't think there's a chance for me to fuck things up further. Allie is refusing to even speak to me."

"Well, you're going to have to figure out how to get past that, or you're going to have to give up." Beck stood and closed his locker. "Those are your two options."

"You say that like it's easy."

"Hell no. It isn't easy." He paused and nodded to one of our teammates as they walked by. He waited until he was around the corner before he spoke again. "But that's your reality. It was the same reality I had to face with Josie. She's either worth the work to get her to forgive you or she isn't, and you're the only one who can decide that."

"But Josie was head over heels in love with you before you fucked everything up."

He nodded his head and crossed his arms. "And Allie was with you. You don't think we all realized that Allie's been into you long before the two of you pushed each other away, then started making your way back to each other? Whatever you did, and I mean beyond that stupid fucking bet, you need to fix it. You need to fix it and make sure she knows that the two of you are worth it."

"And if she doesn't?"

"Make her."

"I don't think Allie can be made to do anything," I grumbled and grabbed my glove. Beck followed me out of the locker room and onto the field.

There were already a couple of our teammates throwing by the time we got out there, but Olly was nowhere to be seen. I pulled my cell phone out of my pocket and sent him a quick text asking him where he was.

Beck and I started throwing, and several minutes later, Olly finally pushed through the locker room door and out onto the field.

He was pissed. I knew that the moment I saw him, and Olly rarely got pissed enough to show his emotions.

"What's wrong?" I asked him as soon as he tossed his baseball bag down on the ground and shoved his left hand in his glove.

"Nothing. Throw me the ball." He hit the inside of his glove, indicating for me to throw it, and I threw the ball to him even though I knew he was lying.

He pulled the ball out of his glove and threw it back to me a lot harder than necessary. I didn't say anything, though. I simply caught the ball, then threw it to Beck. I could see Beck watching Olly too. He knew he was lying just as well as I did.

"Why are your knuckles bloody?" As soon as the question passed Beck's lips, Lucas and Eli walked out onto the field.

I saw Olly wince before I saw anything else. But then I

saw Eli's face. He was pissed too. Angrier than Olly, and he was also sporting a split lip that still had fresh blood pooling around it.

I looked from him to Olly, and I couldn't help noticing how Olly clenched his fist at his side.

"I'm warm," I called to the two of them, even though we had barely thrown, before jogging up beside Olly.

"What the fuck happened?" My question was quiet because the last thing we needed was for Coach to hear us. He would hand us our asses before our practice even began.

"I said, nothing." Olly tried to shrug us off, but neither Beck nor I were having any of that.

"Something happened." I nodded toward Eli who had moved as far from us as he could possibly get to warm up. He looked up in our direction as he ran the back of his hand against his lip. "Did you do that to him?"

"I did." Olly grabbed his bag, and Beck and I followed him to the dugout.

"And?" Beck asked the question we were both thinking.

"And he deserved it. He was talking shit, and I just couldn't stand it anymore." Olly tossed his bag down on the bench.

"Talking shit about what?" I was pretty certain I already knew. If I had to bet, I would say that Eli was talking shit about me or Allie or a combination of the two of us. It was the only thing that guy had to brag about these days.

"Allie," Olly confirmed, and my pulse spiked. "Allie gave him nothing and hasn't spoken to him since that day at the campground, but he's walking around talking like he bagged her. He was telling a few of the guys some bullshit story in the hallway, and I couldn't stand it."

"He was telling people that Allie slept with him?" I could

hear my own anger. I could feel it pulsing through every part of me. This anger was so much easier than the anger I felt toward myself. I could mold it, control it, do something about it.

And I was going to.

"Carson." Beck put his hand on my chest, but I didn't need him to calm me down. I needed Olly to tell me exactly what he said.

"Yeah." Olly nodded, and I knew from the look in his eyes he was thinking about lying to me with what he said next. He realized how easily triggered I was. "But he won't talk about her again. He hit that locker so hard when my fist connected with his jaw that I think he was dazed for a second. He didn't even try to hit me back."

"What the fuck did he say, Olly?" I stared at him because I wasn't fucking around. I wanted to know exactly what that piece of shit was saying about my girl.

"He was just telling them about how you had his sloppy seconds. That he paved the way for you to get inside her."

I didn't wait around to hear another word. I stormed out of the dugout and headed straight for Eli. I didn't care that the rest of the team was still warming up or that Coach was standing there with his clipboard going over our roster. I pushed through all of them until I was face to face with Eli, and he looked up at me with that fucking smirk on his face.

That fucking smirk that was going to get him killed.

"What is it, Hale?" He tossed the ball in the air before catching it back into his mitt. "Are you butt-hurt like your little buddy in there? It's not my fault that Allie dropped your ass after you couldn't give her what she needed."

"Don't say her fucking name again." I stepped toward

him, and there was the slightest flash of fear in his eyes. "Don't talk about her at all."

"What's going on here?" I could hear Coach coming up behind me, but I couldn't care less about him at that moment.

He could punish me however he wanted. He could kick my ass off the team if that's what it took, but I wasn't walking away from Eli until I made it perfectly clear where I stood when it came to Allie.

"Oh shit, my man." Eli laughed and put his hand over his chest. "I thought this was all about a bet. I didn't realize the girl had you fucking whipped."

Laughter rang out around us just as Coach came into view.

"The two of you back away from each other. I don't know what the hell is going on here, but my field isn't the time or place for it."

"Don't tell people that you slept with her when you and I both know that she didn't let you touch her." I didn't know why the thought of him telling everyone bothered me so much. Of course, I didn't want anyone to think badly of Allie, but I also couldn't stand the thought of anyone thinking that she had ever been anyone's other than mine.

"Is that what she told you?" He cocked his head just slightly as if he was analyzing me. "She really is a filthy little whore, isn't she?"

The last words were barely out of his mouth when I barreled into him and tackled him to the ground. My shoulder slammed into his midsection as his back hit the ground, but I didn't have time to think about the ache that already started there. Eli had already thrown his glove to the ground and was throwing punches.

His fist connected with my jaw, then my elbow connected with his nose. After that, it was nothing but a chaos of fists and elbows and jabs and grunts. Eli managed to get himself flipped over me, and he rained down punch after punch into my face and chest.

I barely felt a single one of them.

I caught his fist in my hand and threw a right hook into the side of his head that seemed to stun him. I could hear yelling around us, but I didn't let them stop me. I threw Eli off me, and I continued to throw punches until I felt the crunch of bone beneath my knuckles.

Even then, I didn't stop.

I didn't stop until someone's arms wrapped around my torso and jerked me off of him.

"Fucking stop." Coach's booming voice finally registered then, and I went slack against Beck. "Get him the fuck out of here."

He pointed toward me, and one of the assistant coaches moved in my direction. I shrugged Beck off of me and held up my hands when they looked like they thought I might attack again.

Eli was sitting up and he shoved one of the guys off him that was trying to help him up.

"Remember what I said, Eli." I walked backward away from him in the direction that the assistant coach was leading me. "You talk about her again, and I'll finish wrecking that face of yours."

"Carson, shut your mouth." Coach pointed at me, and his face was so red that he looked like he would have a heart attack at any moment. "You're about to find your ass riding the bench for the rest of the year."

"I don't give a fuck." I looked him in the eye because I

didn't. I knew that baseball was important and that I had scholarships to play in college, but none of it mattered at that moment. I couldn't see past anything but Allie and Eli and the thought of him touching her.

I would give up everything to make sure that he never spoke of her or touched her again.

CHAPTER 3

ALLIE

I walked through the hallway of my school, and I could feel people looking at me. At first, I thought it was in my head, but then I overheard some girls talking about me in the bathroom.

The news of the bet had made it all the way to Clermont High, and I obviously wasn't the only victim of the bet. There were a few other girls from High and several from Prep, but apparently, the bet that involved me specifically was a little more interesting than the others.

And I had heard it all so far. Both Eli and Carson had managed to sleep with me before the bet's time limit, neither of them had, and I even heard one guy whispering that he had heard it ended in a threesome.

I couldn't do anything but roll my eyes.

I had no idea where these people got their information, but none of it could be further from the truth. I hadn't even spoken to Eli since I left that campground even though he had text me to apologize on multiple occasions.

I didn't reply to a single one of them.

Because his apologies didn't matter one way or another to me. Not when I was so focused on Carson.

And I knew that wasn't fair. They were equally guilty in entering the bet. If what Carson said was true, Eli was even more so, but I didn't trust Eli. I didn't care about him.

"Hey, Allie." I looked up from my phone to see Will Hollis leaning next to my locker. He had his thumbs hooked in the straps of his backpack, and he looked nervous. Will was nice. He always had been, but I hated how my stomach dropped seeing him there.

"Hey, Will. What's up?" I opened my locker and shoved my books in before grabbing the ones I needed for my homework tonight.

"I just wanted to check on you." He lowered his voice and leaned in closer to me. "The shit I've been hearing around school has been pretty rough."

"Most of it isn't true." I shrugged and tried to play the whole situation off. "But thank you for checking on me."

"You're welcome." He turned toward me and crossed his arms. "You should come out this weekend. We're planning on having a party down on the north beach."

I nodded my head because I used to go to the beach parties all the time, but it had been a while since I had been to one. "I'll think about it. I just have a lot going on."

"No. I get it." He smiled. "Is work busy as hell right now?"

"Work's busy, trying to keep my grades up, then finishing out my community service."

"I heard about that." He laughed. "I was a little shocked to find out that you are the one who got in trouble, but hey, we all have our wild streaks."

"Not a wild streak." I smiled and closed my locker. "It was just a major lapse in judgment."

"We've all been there." He held up his hand for a high five, and I couldn't help smiling as I slapped my hand against his.

Will was so damn wholesome and nice, and he didn't have to be. He was also hot, incredibly so, and I had no idea how he was still single. He should have been scooped up long before now.

"You know where the party is but text me if you need anything." He shot a finger gun at me, and I laughed as I hiked my bag onto my shoulder and turned in the other direction.

"Maybe she's sleeping with all three of them," I heard a girl whisper from across the hall, and I told myself to ignore it. It didn't matter what they thought of me. I knew the truth.

And that truth was so much sadder than any of them realized.

"I wouldn't put it past her," another snickered, and my spine straightened. I used to be friends with these girls, or at least friendly enough. But people were quick to drop you when they thought they knew you better than you knew yourself. They had heard a few stupid rumors and suddenly they were all experts.

But they forgot that I already knew some of their secrets. Secrets that they had told me themselves. Secrets I would never share because I wasn't like them. I would never be like them.

I pushed outside of the school and took a deep breath as I walked to my car. I was due to be at community service in an hour and a half, but I needed to do something, anything to take the edge off the rising panic that was filling inside of me.

Knowing that I was going to see Carson soon did that to

me because I didn't know what to expect. I had been avoiding him as much as I could while we were there. I absolutely refused to speak to him, but he didn't care.

He was far from ignoring me.

I felt like he watched every single move I made.

I hadn't seen him in a couple days. He had baseball practice yesterday which got us both out of community service, and even though I was dreading seeing him now, I would be lying if I said that I enjoyed being away from him.

It was like my own personal hell.

I wanted to be around him almost as much as I wanted to avoid him. But I guess it had been like that with Carson for a really long time.

I rolled down my windows and let the air rush through my hair. It felt good. It was finally starting to cool down, and I soaked in the feel of the breeze mixed with the warm glow of the sun as I drove away from my school.

I drove and I drove, and by the time I actually looked down at the clock again, I was almost late.

Carson was already there by the time I arrived, but that had become the norm. He was always here working away when I arrived. He acted like he actually took this seriously, like he actually cared what Mr. Sneed thought.

Even though Mr. Sneed didn't give us any indication over whether or not he was happy with the work we were doing or if he planned on letting us stop any time soon. I think the old man had half a mind to keep us working as long as he could get away with it.

Carson didn't say anything as I walked into the house. He was on his knees near the door, and he was sanding the old antique baseboards that were covered in years' worth of paint. I set my bag down on the stairs and watched him as he worked.

He didn't utter a word or so much as look in my direction, and I should have been happy. This was what I had been wanting for days, but it didn't feel like what I wanted.

His shirt was clinging to his back with sweat, and he was sanding the board down like it had personally pissed him off. I grabbed the other block of sandpaper and dropped to my knees beside him. He kept working like he didn't notice my presence at all.

I ran my sandpaper over the wood and tried to ignore him like he was ignoring me, but I couldn't. I looked up at him, and it was then that I noticed his black eye and swollen bottom lip.

I dropped the sandpaper and reached out for him before I thought better of it and caught myself. My hand was so close to his face, and he finally looked up at me then.

His eye was worse than I thought. The bruising went down onto his cheekbone, and there was so much swelling that I was surprised his eye wasn't swollen shut.

"What happened to you?" I pulled my hand away before I did something stupid and touched him, and he watched it retreat.

"Had an altercation." His answer was curt.

"I can see that." I cocked my head to the side to get a good look at him. The skin of his knuckles was broken and some of them were bruised, and I hated that he had been in a fight. "With anyone in particular?"

"Do you really want to know?" He spit out the question as he continued to sand, and I was shocked by his anger.

"I wouldn't have asked if I didn't want to know. Who did that to you?" I pointed to his eye.

"Well, technically you could say I did it to myself since I was the one who threw the first punch, but this black eye I'm sporting is courtesy of your little boyfriend."

"You got in a fight with Eli?" I don't know why that shocked me so much, but it did.

"Of course, you knew exactly who I was talking about," he grumbled.

"Don't be a baby." I looked down at his knuckles. "You know good and well that he's not my boyfriend."

"Does everyone else know that?" He finally looked up at me again.

"What the heck is that supposed to mean?" I didn't care what anyone else knew, and he usually didn't either.

He dropped his sandpaper to the ground and stood. He was covered in dust, and it fell around him as he started pacing the room. "It means that he's telling everyone at school that the two of you slept together."

"Okay?" I had heard the rumor too, but I didn't know that it had come straight from the ass's mouth.

"Okay?" Carson laughed without a trace of humor. "So did you sleep with him?"

"Are you seriously asking me that?" I stood and faced him.

"Yes. I am." He crossed his arms, and if I didn't know him so well, I would have been intimidated. But this version of Carson was the broken boy that I had known for longer than any other version of him. He was insecure and latching on to whatever truth made the most sense to him. Whatever truth he expected other people to let him down with.

"No. I didn't sleep with him, you asshole." I turned on my heel and headed toward the door, but he stopped me with his hand on mine.

"I didn't mean—"

"What, Carson?" I looked back at him over my shoulder. "You didn't mean to assume that I slept with another guy right after I gave you my virginity or that I had lied to you and slept with him before?"

"I didn't think you slept with him at all." His fingers tightened around mine almost to the point of pain. "I just got so fucking angry listening to the shit he said, and it started fucking with my head."

"What Eli says doesn't matter. I don't care what he says about me."

"But I do." He looked so lost in that moment, so at odds with the normal, cocky Carson I had become used to. "I can't stand the thought of other people thinking that he had touched you, that he had been inside you."

I jerked my hand out of his and stepped away as I turned to face him. "I'm not some fucking trophy, Carson. It's not going to tarnish your precious reputation if people think someone else fucked something that you believe once belonged to you."

"I don't give a shit about my reputation."

"Don't you?" I was becoming so angry that part of me was happy he got that black eye. "Why else would you start a fight with Eli? You two had a bet and you won. Congratulations, Carson."

He took a step toward me before stopping himself. "I got in a fight with him because I hate that he even had a chance at touching you. I hate that he kissed you. I hate that I agreed to that stupid fucking bet to begin with." He stepped closer to me again. "I hate that I ever gave him the chance to hurt you."

"He didn't hurt me." I looked him over, and I wished that

he knew what he had always meant to me. I wished that we could go back and change the way our future had become. "You are the one who accomplished that."

"And I told you that I'm sorry."

"My sorrys have never been good enough for you, so what makes you think yours will ever be good enough for me?" I hated that truth, but I couldn't hide it either.

He had hated me for so long and for much less than what he did to me.

He stormed toward me, and I didn't have time to think let alone move before he pressed against me and backed me into the wall. I tried to catch my breath as his battered hand cupped my cheek.

"You know that's not true." He shook his head. "I've been so fucked up, Allie, and I shouldn't have ever put any of that on you."

I could barely swallow as he spoke, and he ran his hand over my neck and followed the movement. I could feel my pulse beating rapidly beneath his fingers. "It doesn't matter."

"Yes. It does." He leaned in closer to me, and I didn't move away.

It was stupid and reckless, but I couldn't move away from him. Not when he was like this. He pressed his lips to mine, gently at first, then more harshly. It was as if that first touch set off a frenzy inside of him.

He kissed me like he had missed every inch of me. His hand tightened on my neck and the other tangled into my hair. I kissed him back just as hard.

I put every bit of anger and hurt into the kiss, and I hoped he felt it. I hoped that he knew this wasn't some kiss that was going to make things better for us. I wasn't sure that even existed.

There wasn't anything that could take back the things that had been done.

His teeth pressed into my bottom lip before he sucked it into his mouth, and I couldn't stop the small whimper that passed my lips.

There was an ache deep in my belly, an ache that only he had ever fixed, and I hated that one simple kiss could make me want him so badly. My legs trembled beneath me, and my heart felt like it didn't even belong to me.

As much as I hated him, I was still so turned on by him. I wanted him regardless of everything that happened.

He pressed his hips into mine, and I felt how badly he wanted me too. It would be so easy to forget everything and give into each other. I didn't need some grand gesture of love for me to fall apart under Carson's hands, but I also knew that I couldn't keep things separate either. The moment he touched me, him touching me now, it messed with my heart.

My chest ached as badly as the low ache in my stomach. My body was completely at war with itself.

If I gave into Carson now, I would hate him even more later. I would hate myself. Because no matter what happened or what he felt, I was in love with Carson Hale, and I was only at risk of falling deeper and deeper for him.

I was going to continue to fall, and he wouldn't. I would fall and it would shred me apart.

Because Carson wasn't the kind of guy I was meant to fall for. He wasn't some knight in shining armor who was going to give me my happily ever after. I used to think he was, but I was so damn foolish.

The boy I used to daydream about and the boy touching me now were two different people. They were night and day, and I needed to draw the line of who he is and who he was in my head.

Right now, everything was muddy and nothing about us was clear, and every time I allowed something like this to happen, it only became worse.

I pushed against his chest, and Carson reluctantly pulled away from me. His breathing was harsh and mingled with mine, and he looked as lost as I was.

"We can't do this." My voice was barely a whisper between us, but it felt so heavy on my tongue.

"Allie." He caressed my cheek, but I pulled away.

"No." I pushed harder against him and didn't look back as I walked away from him and out of the old house.

CHAPTER 4
CARSON

We walked into the country club, and I knew she was there. Her car was parked outside, along with Josie's, and Olly had tried to talk us into going somewhere else.

When we took a seat in the restaurant, it was all I could do to search every inch of the space looking for her, but I didn't see her anywhere.

"I can't believe Coach benched you. How long did he say again?" Beck asked.

"Two weeks." I heard the kitchen door open and looked toward it, but it wasn't her.

"That seems a bit harsh, but I guess it could be a lot worse."

"Yeah." Olly nodded. "You're lucky he kept it between the team. The school would have probably suspended you both."

"What about you?" Beck nodded toward Olly.

"No one saw us." Olly chuckled. "I didn't make a grand event out of it like Carson."

They both chuckled and I rolled my eyes. "It's not like I was planning it. Actually, I should really blame it on you. If you hadn't come to practice so pissed, I wouldn't have even gotten in trouble, asshole."

"Okay," Olly said sarcastically and leaned back in his chair. "I had just defended your girl's honor, but please, blame it on me."

I was obviously joking, but when I looked over at him, I realized that I never did thank him for that. "You're right." I held out my fist, and he bumped his against it. "Thank you for that."

"No problem. I doubt Eli will be talking shit again anytime soon."

"I don't know." Beck was checking his phone but put it down on the table. "He seems like a pretty big idiot, and he's friends with Lucas. God knows he's not going to be making any smart decisions."

"This is true," I said just as Josie walked up to the table.

"Hey, guys." She grinned down at Beck. "What can I get you all to drink?"

Beck grabbed the edge of her apron and pulled her toward him. He didn't give her any time to object as he pulled her down and pressed his lips to hers.

"Beck," she huffed and straightened. "I'm at work."

"So?" He looked up at her like she was crazy.

"So, I'd like to not get fired."

We all chuckled because we knew that was never going to happen. Even if Beck's dad didn't own the place, Josie was a good worker and Mr. Clermont adored her.

"Now what do you all want to drink?"

"Water."

"Same," Olly answered.

"Is Allie here?" I leaned back in my chair and wished I never opened my big mouth.

Josie narrowed her eyes at me. "She is."

I nodded and tried to appear disinterested, but I wasn't fooling anyone. "Like, in the restaurant?"

Josie grinned this time before she spoke. "The last time I saw her she was back there in the kitchen making out with the hot new cook we got."

Beck swatted at her leg, and she grimaced. "Ow."

I knew she was fucking with me, but my heart still raced at her words.

"Don't fuck around, Josie. He just got benched for fighting for her honor. I'd hate to see what he'd do if he actually caught another guy touching her." Olly looked over at me. "He's volatile now that she broke his heart."

"She didn't break my heart," I grumbled, and they all three of them looked at me like they didn't believe a single word I said.

"Didn't she?" Josie put her hands on her hips. "From the outside looking in, it looks like the two of you broke each other's hearts."

"Well, since you're so knowledgeable, do you think I have even the slightest chance of fixing things?"

"I don't know." She watched me. "And I honestly don't know if I want you to. You've been a complete and total jerk to her."

"I know." We all did.

"And then you somehow convinced her to like you again after you've treated her like shit for as long as I've known you."

"Yeah."

"Then you broke her again."

"I didn't mean to. I…"

"It doesn't matter what you meant to do. It's what happened, and clinging to the fact that it's not what you intended to happen is going to get you nowhere. If you want to get her back, you need to prove that you aren't this asshole that you've made her believe you are."

"I thought you didn't want me to get her back."

"I said I didn't know." She pointed at me. "I'm not sure if I trust you with her again."

"But you're going to give me a chance?"

"It's not my chance to give. I will stand by whatever decision Allie makes. If she says you're a piece of shit, then you're a piece of shit."

"Okay." I chuckled. "That's fair."

"But, if you hurt her again, I swear on my life that Beck is going to kick your ass."

I looked over at my best friend as he winced.

"Deal. If I hurt her again, I will gladly get my ass kicked by him."

"Good." She took a step back. "Now let me go get your drinks."

As soon as she walked away, I spotted Allie behind the bar. She was laughing with the bartender as she placed some drinks onto her tray. She looked so damn beautiful.

Her hair was tied back away from her face, and she was in her plain uniform that the rest of the staff wore. But it didn't look plain on her. It looked anything but.

She lifted the tray in her hand and laughed as she walked away from the bar. She hadn't looked up at me, and I didn't know if she was aware I was here. I figured Josie would have told her, warned her, but she was walking through the restaurant like she didn't have a care in the world.

And it could simply be that she didn't care that I was here at all, but I had to believe that wasn't it.

After I kissed her at community service yesterday, she looked so torn, so hurt, and I wanted to do anything I possibly could to take that look away from her. But she didn't give me a chance. She ran before I could say or do anything.

I had told Mr. Sneed that she had gotten sick. I knew that he didn't believe me. He made that perfectly clear, but I had stayed an extra hour to make up for her being gone.

She went to a table a few away from us, and she smiled at the guests as she sat their alcohol down in front of them. I watched her as she worked. She was so good at her job, so friendly and personable, and it made me wonder what she was going to go on to do.

Allie was capable of doing or being whatever it was she wanted, but I didn't think she believed that. I had probably helped plant any seeds of doubt that she had.

And I wished that I could take every second of that away.

I wished that I could take back so much of what I had done and said, but I couldn't. The only thing I could do now was be different for her, but I didn't know if I was capable of that.

She walked away from the table and her steps faltered when her gaze finally landed on me. She looked around the table quickly before storming toward where I sat.

"What are you doing here?" she hissed, and I knew that she was still pissed about yesterday or everything that happened before yesterday. Either way, she wasn't happy to see me.

"Eating dinner." I motioned around us as if that fact should have been obvious. That only pissed her off more.

"There are a hundred different restaurants in this town. Couldn't you all have found somewhere else to go?"

"In all fairness, my dad owns this place, so we come here a lot."

Allie's gaze snapped to Beck, and he quickly shut up.

"I didn't realize that you worked tonight," I lied to her. "I also didn't realize that it was such a big issue for you to see me."

"Well, now you know." She tucked the tray she was carrying under her arm. "I'm already forced to do community service with you. You could at least give me a night off."

"Forced?" I raised an eyebrow at her, and I knew I should have stopped talking, but getting a rise out of her was so entertaining and such a damn turn on. "I thought you were enjoying our time together."

"Wrong." Her answer was instant.

Josie walked up behind her and looked back and forth between us before sitting our drinks on the table.

"You didn't enjoy what happened yesterday?"

"What happened yesterday?" Josie asked, and I watched as Allie's face reddened.

"Nothing happened."

"It most certainly did." I looked back and forth between them. "Allie might be pissed at me, but she didn't stop me from kissing her."

"That's a lie. I did stop you."

"After you thoroughly enjoyed it." God, it had felt like she enjoyed it.

"Then I came to my senses and realized that I was kissing the asshole who had just broke me." Her fist was clenched at her side, and she was staring directly at me. "Don't worry. I will never let it happen again."

"It will." I said it with so much power because I truly meant it. I would do whatever it took to make sure it did.

"No. It won't." She finally looked away from me and around the table. "Go ahead and make bets about it if you need to. It's not going to happen."

Then she stormed away from the table and back to the kitchen.

Josie sighed, and I looked away from Allie's retreating form to look up at her. "I had, like, the tiniest bit of faith that you could pull this off, but you lost that. If you all take bets, put me down for a hundred on him not getting the girl."

Then she flipped me off.

CHAPTER 5
ALLIE

I was pissed.

More than pissed, actually. I was so angry that I couldn't think straight and spending another day alone with Carson was the absolute last thing I wanted to do.

Because I knew that getting under my skin had become a dang game to him.

He pushes and pushes until I can't take anymore, then he laps up my anger like it's a damn drug to him.

I managed to get to community service before he arrived, and I was glad. I didn't have the energy to deal with him or avoid talking to him as I tried to start whatever job Mr. Sneed wanted us to do today.

I walked up to the front door, and there was a note taped to it. I rolled my eyes at Mr. Sneed's writing, where he thanked Carson for something he had done to the original woodwork before asking us to start working on the kitchen.

I left the note where it was so Carson could see it, then I walked into the house. It was pretty creepy without Carson here, but there was no way in hell I was going to stand there and wait on him and give him any sort of ammunition over me. No. I was just going to pull up my big girl panties, check behind me every five seconds, and get to work.

I was doing exactly that by the time Carson walked in. He was singing the lyrics to some song I didn't know, and I tried to ignore him as I used the broom to sweep all the cobwebs that covered almost every inch of the forgotten kitchen.

"Hello." Carson's friendly tone made my back straighten and my heart race.

I nodded in his direction but didn't respond. My heart was racing, but I tried not to let it show.

"Okay." He chuckled and turned away from me. He started working. I had no idea what he was doing, but I also didn't care. I wasn't here to worry about Carson or the way he may or may not have made me feel. Or what it was like when I kissed him the other day.

Nope. I definitely wasn't here to think about kissing him again.

It wasn't running through my mind over and over and tying my stomach into knots.

"Did someone piss you off?" Finally, he looked back up at me.

I wasn't thinking as I moved toward him and shoved against his chest. My fingers trembled along with my nerves. Dealing with Carson Hale was no longer something I wanted to do. I was so tired of his game of hot and cold. I was so exhausted trying to figure out what he wanted and didn't want from me.

"Allie," he said my name and made it sound like more

than it was. I pushed him again, forcing his back to hit the wall in the hallway because that only pissed me off more. I felt that one simple word like it was racing through me, chasing something I didn't have. "Fuck. Stop hitting me."

"I'm not hitting you," I hissed the words between my teeth because I wanted to hit him. I wanted to take every bit of aggression I felt out on him because it was all his fault.

He snatched my hand in his before I could push him again and held it against his chest. "What do you call that then?"

I tried to tug my hand back from him, but he refused to let go. He held my hand firmly against his chest as he scowled down at me. Every bit of the playfulness from earlier was gone.

"I call it pushing you away." I tilted my head to the side and stared at him. "You should recognize that from a mile away. You're the king of it, aren't you?"

Finally, there was a trace of a smile on his lips, and it was all I needed to flame my anger. He was so damn cocky and sure that he was exactly what everyone else wanted, but he was wrong.

I wanted nothing to do with him. Not anymore. Not after everything happened and still continued to mess with my head. He made me weak, and I refused to be that girl anymore.

I refused to allow him to use me and my heart as nothing more than a toy for him to play with.

Because that was exactly what I had been all along.

"You're the one who has been pushing me away lately, remember?"

"No." I shook my head and tugged on my hand again. "I

remember you being a complete and total asshole and ruining anything that might have happened between us."

"You mean, what did happen between us."

"No. I meant everything that you faked. Nothing that happened was real. None of it mattered." My chest ached as I spoke the words, but I knew they were true. As badly as I wished they weren't, that was my reality.

I had handed things over to Carson that he didn't deserve. He played me and I fell into it effortlessly. It didn't matter what he said about Eli. Carson was the devil in disguise. He was the one who burned me so damn easily without even trying.

Eli never stood a chance.

Not against him.

"Don't say that." He jerked my hand closer and forced my feet to stumble forward toward him. My other hand pressed against his chest to try to maintain distance between us. I couldn't risk being so close to him that I couldn't keep my head clear.

Being close to him did more than just mess with my head. It messed with every single part of me. My heart raced and I felt like I was falling. He was like my center of gravity and no matter how badly I wished he wasn't, I was drawn to him.

It didn't matter what he did or said or how badly he treated me, I was drawn to him in a way that I couldn't explain or couldn't deny.

And I hated it.

"Why wouldn't I say that? It's the truth."

He shook his head before bringing his gaze back to me. "No. It's not. Everything we have is real. That stupid fucking bet doesn't matter."

"You don't get to decide that." I jerked away from him again, and this time I slipped from his grip. "You made that bet without a single thought about how I would feel. You didn't care that you made me look like a fool."

"Really?" He pushed his hands through his hair and pushed off the wall. "The only reason I said yes to that bet was because I give a shit about you. Do you really think I would do anything with Lucas if not? Do you think I would stoop to his level?"

"I didn't." I was honest with him because as much as I hated Carson at that moment, he still would never be anything like Lucas. "But you've proven to be exactly who you are again and again. You are not the boy who used to be my best friend."

"You're right." He swallowed so hard I could see the force of his Adam's apple pushing against his throat. "I am not him, and I will never be him again. Is that what you want? Do you want me to go back to that pathetic kid who didn't have a fucking clue about the world?"

His words were so harsh as he watched me, and they felt like a rough caress against my skin.

"I want you to go back to the guy who didn't need to be all this." I waved my hand in his direction. "I want you to go back to being the guy who wasn't more concerned with getting into girls' pants than he was with breaking their hearts."

"Is that all you think this was?" He laughed and a chill ran down my spine. "Me trying to get into your pants?"

"You succeeded. Didn't you?" I crossed my arms and stood my ground. My chest was heaving, and my heart raced, but I hoped he didn't notice either. I hoped he didn't see how affected I was by every little thing he said or did.

"I think I did more than succeed." He stepped closer to me, and I took a step back. My heels bumped into the baseboard before my back hit the wall. "I gave you more of myself than I've ever given to anyone else, Allie. If that doesn't mean anything to you, then fine, but it means something to me."

He searched my eyes, and I tried to calm down. "Because you kissed me?"

He laughed again and shook his head. "Because I kissed you, because I..." he hesitated, and I held my breath for his next words.

"What, Carson? What did you do?"

"I have been trying to hold myself back. I was dying every second that I was touching you to tell you that..." He hesitated again and searched my eyes. This time I let him. I let him have whatever time he needed to work out what was going on in that fucked-up head of his. "I love you, Allie."

His words should have thrilled me. I had been waiting for those words for as long as I could remember, but now they felt like a weapon.

Just another tool in his arsenal that he could use to destroy me.

Carson Hale didn't love me.

He had no idea what love was.

And it wasn't the idea of him not loving me that made me feel like I was breaking. It was the thought that I ever held onto any hope at all.

That sliver of hope that I tried to pretend wasn't there had been my downfall all along.

"Don't say things like that." My voice was far too shaky, and I hated that I allowed him to see that weakness.

"I mean it."

"No." I shook my head as the anger built inside me. "You don't. You don't ever mean the things you say."

"Allie, I don't know what you want me to say." He sounded just as frustrated as I did, but I didn't care. I could no longer be a doormat for him. I refused to be exactly like the rest of the girls he was used to running all over. Even if I had been exactly that up until this point. "What do you want me to do?"

"Leave me alone." I stared at him, and the ache in my chest became deeper. My words felt like a lie. They were a lie, but I knew that was what I needed. It didn't matter what I wanted from him. What I wanted and what I needed were as opposite as the two of us.

The things I wanted from him got me hurt. The things I needed did too, but it was different. It was the kind of hurt that I could protect myself with. The kind of hurt that I could use to make sure he wouldn't break my heart again in this lifetime.

"You don't mean that." He searched my face, and I knew I needed to get out of here. He looked so desperate, so scared of what I would say next, and I hated it. I hated that every part of me wanted to take that look away from him. I wanted to assure him that I would give him whatever he wanted from me.

But that was the problem.

If I didn't put distance between us, I would. I would give him everything, and he would take it.

And I would be left with nothing.

"I do." I moved to get past him, but he leaned into me, his body pressing against mine.

"I'm sorry." He choked out the words near my ear, and everything inside me felt like it was at war with itself.

I was so confused, so tired, and I didn't know how to answer him.

I didn't know how to stay away from him when everything made me feel like I was being pulled back.

"For what?" I turned my face to look at him, and our lips were so close to each other. His breath feathered against my lips as his chest rose and fell against mine, and even though I wanted to hate the feel of all of it, I didn't.

It felt like I was exactly where I was meant to be.

"For everything." He looked so hesitant as he spoke. "I'm sorry about the bet. I'm sorry that you think that what happened between us was fake. I'm sorry that I've been treating you like shit for a really long time."

"Carson." I shook my head.

"It's the truth. I've been a damn fool, and I'm sorry." He gripped my side in his hand, his fingers digging into me, and I didn't stop him.

"I don't forgive you."

His fingers tightened against me. "I don't expect you to."

"Then what do you expect? What do you want?" It was the question I was dying for him to answer and for him to finally give me some truth. I needed to know what he was going to take from me next, what I was going to give.

"I want you to forgive me even though you shouldn't. I want you to give me another chance." His voice was soft and like a caress over my skin.

"I can't." I looked away from him, but he reached out and caught my chin with his other hand.

"Please, Allie." His lips were pressed against my skin as

he spoke, and they broke through every barrier I had against him.

I couldn't just give him everything he wanted. I couldn't let him take everything I had to give, but I also couldn't walk away from him. Not in that moment when he was looking at me like I was the only thing that would take all his demons away.

He didn't deserve me, but I would give another piece of myself to him regardless.

I had no choice.

I didn't answer him because I knew he wouldn't like what I had to say. What I was giving him wasn't another chance, it was another moment. It was a moment that we both needed. A moment that I couldn't deny.

I turned to face him more, and I gently pressed my lips against his. He let out a harsh breath and his hands tightened against me.

He held me there for only a moment before his control seemed to snap and he buried his hand in my hair. His hold was painful, but I didn't want him to loosen it. My body begged for more.

His mouth slammed down against mine, and his kiss was frantic and wild. I could taste his hope on my lips and his desperation on my tongue. This was no longer a game to him. He wanted me as much as I had wanted him for years, and he was no longer the one who was in control.

Not really.

His teeth nipped against my bottom lip before he sucked it into his mouth, and I brought my hands to his shoulders to hold myself steady. As much as I wanted to hate him, my body still wanted him. I wanted everything I knew he could give me.

He kissed down my chin and along my jaw before moving to my neck. My hips jolted forward against his as his tongue tasted every inch of skin he passed. Every part of me felt like it was on edge, begging for his touch yet wholly unprepared.

"I need to taste you," he murmured against my skin before dropping to his knees in front of me.

He didn't wait for my answer before he lifted my shirt and pressed his mouth to my stomach. His tongue ran over my belly button as his fingers worked my shorts down my hips.

He was wasting no time. There were no pretenses about what either of us wanted. He ran his nose over the softness of my stomach before looking up at me. He didn't take his gaze away from mine as he pressed his mouth over my panties.

I tensed and bit down on my bottom lip. I was so ready, so desperate for him to give me more.

His fingers were spread wide as he pushed them up along my thighs, but they were so sure once they reached my panties. He jerked them down my legs until they fell to my feet with my shorts.

He was no longer looking up at me. He was staring straight ahead at my pussy, and I tried to breathe as I watched him.

I should have stopped him. Logically, I knew that, but I couldn't. I would face whatever consequences I had to face. I would deal with the heartbreak I knew I would feel when I walked out of here, but I just needed this rush he gave me.

If only for a moment, I needed to feel his hands on me and to pretend like nothing else mattered but the two of us.

It was a lie I was more than willing to believe for the

moment. A taste of his lies was far better than the truth. His lies were better than anything else I had ever experienced.

He slid his tongue against me before groaning. "God, you are so fucking wet."

I couldn't bring myself to be embarrassed. Instead, I lifted my foot and kicked off my clothes from around my ankles to give him better access to my body.

He lifted my thigh in his hand before I could get my foot back to the ground and put it over his shoulder. I was so open, so exposed in front of him, but he didn't lift his head away from my pussy for even a moment.

He dove into me. His mouth licking, sucking, and nipping at my flesh. I pushed even closer to him as I buried my hands in his hair. I was on my tiptoes with my head thrown back against the wall, and I felt like I was barely hanging on by a thread.

I could fall at any moment, and he would be the only thing I had to hold me up. He was the person I should have trusted least in the world, but I knew that even now that wasn't true.

"Carson," I called out his name because I already felt so close to an orgasm.

"You taste so good." His words vibrated against my pussy as his hand dug into my hip. "This pussy is mine, Allie. Do you hear me?"

I nodded even though we both knew what we were saying didn't really matter, but he growled at my answer. He lifted my other foot from the ground, gripping my thigh in his hand, and he rested it against his other shoulder.

I was in the air, my back against the wall, the weight of me resting on his shoulders, and he barely seemed to notice.

He ate me harder as his hands dug into my ass, tugging me closer to his mouth.

"Oh, God. Yes." I held on to him for dear life as I moved against him. I couldn't stop myself. My hips rolled against his face, and it only seemed to spur him on.

He sucked my clit into his mouth, and I slammed my head back against the wall. My orgasm rolled through me, the feeling racing through every corner of my body. Carson had complete control over me. I didn't know where I began and he ended. I didn't know how I was still leaning upright against the wall.

I could feel him moving beneath me before he pulled me away from the wall, and I grabbed onto his shoulders as he moved me down his body.

"Where are we going?" My voice was so sleepy and satisfied as he carried me.

"I need to get inside you," he growled against my neck. "I feel like I'm dying." He laid me down against the staircase. My ass hit the stairs before my shoulder blades pressed against the ones above it. Carson kneeled between my thighs, and he stared up at me as he quickly unbuttoned his jeans.

He paused just as he pulled out his cock, and he stared up at me. "We can't do this."

"What do you mean?" I leaned forward and wrapped my hand around him. He leaned forward into my touch, and I ran his cock against me. He slid through my wetness, back and forth from my clit to my opening, and I was dying for him to push inside me.

I had just come, but I wanted more. I was desperate to feel him inside me. I needed it.

"Allie." My name sounded painful on his lips. "I wasn't expecting this. I didn't bring a condom."

I heard what he said, but there was no rational thinking left in my brain. I didn't care about the stupid condom.

"Don't come inside me." I leaned back again and lifted my shirt to expose my stomach and breasts. "Come here." I ran my fingers over my skin and to my breast. I pinched my nipple between my fingers as he watched me.

"I've never." He shook his head. "I've never fucked anyone without a condom. I'm clean."

"Me neither." I smiled at him, and his lips tugged up on the side. I pinched my nipple again and I could feel the ricochet of my orgasm throughout my body. I tightened my thighs around Carson's hips before sliding my other hand down my body.

He was still watching me, and I couldn't take another second of it. I needed more. I slid my fingers over my clit and cried out at the feeling.

"Are you going to make me fuck myself?" I asked him before I thought better of it, and I could feel my embarrassment creeping in. I had never been so forward with Carson, with anyone.

"Fucking hell." Carson moved over me, and his mouth slammed against my mouth. He lined himself up before sliding into me with one long push. It felt so different than the last time, so much easier, but there was still a bite of pain.

"Oh, God." I wrapped my hand around the back of his neck as he began moving inside me.

He had one of my thighs in his hand, spreading me open for him, and he didn't stop kissing me. Not even for a moment.

My pussy clenched around him. I was still so sensitive from when he just ate me, and I already felt like I was on the brink of another orgasm.

"Nothing has ever felt this good." His words rushed out against my mouth, and even though I told myself not to believe him, every word felt like a shot to my chest. "This is what it should have always been."

Don't let him fuck with your head, Allie.

He lifted off me, moving to the stair at my side, and he grabbed for me. He pulled me over him until my thighs were straddling his, and he lowered me back down on him. He felt so much deeper like this.

I pushed my hands into his shoulders as I stared down at where we connected as I began to move. He gripped my ass in his hands and lifted me slightly before letting me fall back down against him.

Over and over, he helped me until I got the hang of the rhythm he set, then I took over. I rode him as he lifted my shirt and cupped my breasts in his hands. His fingers rolled over my nipples before his mouth pressed against the fabric of my bra.

The feel of him so deep inside me combined with the torturous gentleness of his mouth and hands was too much. I stared down at him as I rode him, and I didn't see the Carson who was capable of breaking my heart at every turn. I saw the Carson that I had fallen in love with a long time ago.

The one I couldn't seem to shake no matter how hard I tried.

I kept the pace as my heart thundered in my chest almost violently. He clung to me as if he was worried I would disappear at any moment, and I held him because I knew that fact to be true.

My orgasm coursed through my body, this one unbelievably stronger than the last, and I cried out his name. He didn't stop moving beneath me. He gripped my neck in his hand and forced my mouth down to meet his.

His kiss felt like a promise that I didn't believe, his hands a vow that I couldn't accept.

I tried to shield myself from both, but it was futile.

They flooded me without my permission. They suffocated me despite my armor.

"Oh, God, Allie." Carson's words were rushed and frantic, and I felt him come inside me only moments after I fell over the edge.

His arms were wrapped around me, and my forehead was pressed against his. I didn't have the courage to open my eyes yet or to utter a word. I just sat there and tried to calm my masochistic heart.

I could feel him shift beneath me, and the proof of the mistake we had just made leaked down my inner thighs. It was enough to make me come to my senses.

I climbed off of him before he could stop me, and I quickly grabbed my clothing from the ground. I glanced up at him long enough to see the panic in his eyes, but I didn't linger there. I couldn't.

"Allie." I heard him call my name, but I didn't stop. I finished getting dressed without even taking a moment to clean up, and I searched for my purse so I could leave.

"Baby. Please, stop."

I spun around to face him, and he was jerking his pants back up his hips. "I am not your baby."

I tried not to think about the look on his face as I walked away and made my way to the door. I could feel him following me, but I knew I couldn't stop. If I stopped for him, I knew I wouldn't be able to walk away.

"Please don't leave, Allie."

Every part of me wanted to turn around and stay, but I couldn't. I wouldn't survive him again. So, I did the one thing I knew he was the master of, I walked away.

THANK YOU

Thank you so much for reading Allie and Carson's story! Their story will continue in The Deceit of a Devil, and I'm so excited for you to read the conclusion of their heartbreaking romance.

This story will take you on a rollercoaster, and I hope that you are enjoying the ride. I'm not sure if my heart has ever hurt more for two characters, and I hope that you'll join me as we piece the two of them back together.

I would love for you to join my reader group, Hollywood, so we can connect and talk about all of your The Taste of an Enemy thoughts. This group is the first place to find out about cover reveals, book news, and new releases!

I would also love for you to sign up for my newsletter!

Again, thank you for going on this wild journey with me.

Xo,
Holly Renee
www.authorhollyrenee.com

Before You Go
Please consider leaving an honest review.